Praise for Jillian Hart

"A sweet romance with characters
who only want the best for one another."
—*RT Book Reviews* on "Her Christmas Family"
in *Mail-Order Christmas Brides*

"A sweet, romantic novel,
with memorable characters."
—*RT Book Reviews* on *Snowflake Bride*

"This is a beautiful love story between two people
from different stations in life, or so it appears."
—*RT Book Reviews* on *Patchwork Bride*

Praise for Janet Tronstad

"This great story filled with kindness,
understanding and love is sure to please."
—*RT Book Reviews*
on "Christmas Stars for Dry Creek"
in *Mail-Order Christmas Brides*

"Elizabeth is a wonderful, caring character.
Jake is a gentle giant,
and their love story is full of Christmas joy."
—*RT Book Reviews* on *Calico Christmas at Dry Creek*

"Janet Tronstad's quirky small town
and witty characters will add warmth
and joy to your holiday season."
—*RT Book Reviews* on
"Christmas Bells for Dry Creek"
in *Mistletoe Courtship*

JILLIAN HART

grew up on her family's homestead, where she helped raise cattle, rode horses and scribbled stories in her spare time. After earning her English degree from Whitman College, she worked in travel and advertising before selling her first novel. When Jillian isn't working on her next story, she can be found puttering in her rose garden, curled up with a good book or spending quiet evenings at home with her family.

JANET TRONSTAD

grew up on her family's farm in central Montana and now lives in Pasadena, California, where she is always at work on her next book. She has written more than thirty books, many of them set in the fictitious town of Dry Creek, Montana, where the men spend the winters gathered around the potbellied stove in the hardware store and the women make jelly in the fall.

Mail-Order Holiday Brides

JILLIAN HART

JANET TRONSTAD

Love Inspired

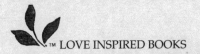

™ LOVE INSPIRED BOOKS

ISBN-13: 978-0-373-82943-9

MAIL-ORDER HOLIDAY BRIDES
Copyright © 2012 by Harlequin Books S.A.

The publisher acknowledges the copyright holders of the individual works as follows:

HOME FOR CHRISTMAS
Copyright © 2012 by Jill Strickler

SNOWFLAKES FOR DRY CREEK
Copyright © 2012 by Janet Tronstad

www.LoveInspiredBooks.com

Printed in U.S.A.

CONTENTS

HOME FOR CHRISTMAS

Jillian Hart

And let the peace of God rule in your hearts.
—*Colossians* 3:15

Chapter One

Montana Territory
December 21, 1885

"I think we've been on this train forever." Christina Eberlee gripped the handrail, breezed down the steps from the passenger car and landed on the icy depot platform. Snowflakes caught on her eyelashes and needled her face as she twirled around in the December wind, waiting for her new friend to descend from the passenger car. "Or at least it feels that way."

"It certainly does," Annabelle Hester agreed, holding her beautiful hat in place as the wind tried to snatch it. "It feels nice to get out in the fresh air. I'm afraid train travel isn't quite as glamorous as I imagined."

"Me, either. Exciting, but cramped. Who would have guessed?" Christina trudged through the snow, thinking of the blessing of Annabelle's companionship. Before they'd met, she'd sat alone on her velvet-covered seat, listening to the clickety-clack of the wheels on steel rails and counting the miles passing by. Dread was a hard thing to battle alone, envisioning all the things that could go wrong with this mail-order bride situation she found herself in.

Her biggest problem would have to be that her imagination would not stop seeing doom. Tom Rutger might be a perfectly fine man—he'd certainly seemed so in the letters they'd exchanged—but her errant mind kept picturing a bald bridegroom with a severe overbite and warts. A man that smelled like cabbage. Or— and this was the worst—one of those men who was nothing but hair, including a gigantic handlebar mustache, bushy beard and hair curling over the backs of his hands like fur.

Then Annabelle Hester had joined her table in the dining car, and Christina was delighted to learn she wasn't the only mail-order bride on board. Annabelle was one, too! Finally, someone who could share her worries. Annabelle had chuckled over Christina's greatest fear—abundantly curling hand hair—and they'd become instant friends.

"Montana Territory is such wide-open country," Annabelle commented as she looked around. She was a dainty, lovely young woman who outshone every other female on the platform. "So different from back East."

"You will come to like it, I'm sure. I didn't like Dakota Territory at first, but I came to love the wide-open spaces and the skies that go on forever. Not that you can see either with all this snow," Christina replied.

"No, as I can hardly see my hand in front of my face. Or you," Annabelle quipped in a dignified manner.

"Are you starting to get excited?" Christina trudged through the near-blizzard conditions toward the depot, where lemony light offered shelter and the promise of warmth. Her teeth were chattering.

"I'm quite looking forward to meeting Adam Stone, my husband-to-be." Annabelle tumbled through the open door. "I'm grateful to find such a man."

"I pray he is a great blessing for your life." The blast of heat from the potbellied stove in the center of the train station's waiting room felt delicious as she looked around. A ticket counter and the telegraph window stood at one end and the newsstand at another. A kindly faced matronly woman was pouring cups of coffee and tea for interested passengers. The little sign said two cents.

And that was two cents too much. Christina's heart sank. Her reticule, dangling from her wrist, didn't have so much as a penny inside it. She'd spent her last few cents on her breakfast toast and tea. Her stomach rumbled, reminding her it was almost noon.

"Are you in the mood for something hot to drink?" Christina asked. "I'll wait in line with you, if you are."

Something—or more accurately someone—crashed into her shoulder. Knocked off balance, she slammed to the floor. Pain roared through her arm. All she saw was a blur racing away—the boy who'd rammed into her, a reticule swinging from his hand.

My reticule, she realized. He has my reticule! She

levered herself up, watching in horror as the kid dashed through the doorway and into the storm.

"Help!" Annabelle called. "Stop that boy!"

But he was gone, just an impression of a dark coat and a faded red hat disappearing into the veil of snow, her most treasured possessions gone with him. A lump wedged into her throat. Vaguely she was aware of footsteps charging the length of the room as a man in a black coat and Stetson raced into the snow.

"Are you all right?" Genuine concern marked Annabelle's lovely face as she grasped Christina by the elbow and helped her up. "Are you hurt? Oh, you're bleeding."

"Am I? It's nothing." At least she was trying to pretend so. Pain shot up her arm in swift, knife-sharp spikes and she gritted her teeth against it. Her worst injury was the loss of the contents of her reticule—her dead adoptive mother's broach and the locket with the image of her sisters, whom she hadn't seen since she was adopted as a small child. Now all she had of her sisters was the fading image in her head.

"Christina, you can deny it all you want, but it doesn't change the facts. You are hurt and you need a doctor. Maybe there's one traveling on the train."

Tears swam into her eyes, but she blinked them away. She cradled her aching arm, standing on shaky knees. Everyone stared at her. How embarrassing. She wanted to sink through a hole in the floor. If only she'd been paying better attention, she might have seen the boy coming.

"Don't you worry," Annabelle soothed. "I don't

have much money, but I'll split what I have with you. It will be enough for meals until you reach Angel Falls."

"That's generous of you, but no, I can't take your money." Especially since she'd run out of her own funds anyway. She swallowed hard, pushing the sharp zing of pain to the back of her mind. It was nothing but a bump, she thought, cradling her hurting arm. Maybe a bruise. No need to worry. She swiped blood away from the skinned heel of her hand.

"Poor dear." A plump older lady gave her a sympathetic look. She patted one of the benches near the stove. "Perhaps you should come sit down here. I sent my daughter to tell the ticket clerk to fetch a doctor."

"No doctor." A medical bill was the last thing she needed. "I can't afford one."

"Maybe that man was able to catch the boy and bring back your reticule," Annabelle said hopefully.

"What man?"

"The one who ran after the boy." Annabelle gestured toward the doorway.

Right. The man had returned, nothing but a blurry shadow cloaked by the thick snowfall on the train platform. The vague shadow took on shape. First a hint of wide shoulders and the crown of a Stetson coming closer until he broke through the storm and everything and everyone surrounding her vanished in comparison. She caught a hint of his face as he strode forcefully into the light—rugged, carved granite, high cheekbones and an iron jaw. At well over six feet, he towered over everyone in the room, a formidable behemoth of a man with a badge glinting on his dark wool coat.

"Sorry, ma'am, he got away from me. He had too big of a head start." His dark blue gaze gentled, softening with apology. An odd combination—steely man and kind heart.

"I figured as much. Thank you for trying."

"I just wish I'd been successful. You've been hurt."

"Nothing to worry about." Or so she was hoping.

"You hit the floor pretty hard." He knelt before her, closing the distance between them. His closeness unsettled her, as if he'd chased off every speck of air in the station. Concern softened the rugged planes of his masculine face. "Can you wiggle your fingers?"

"Can you wiggle yours?" Christina asked.

"As a matter of fact I can." Seriousness clung to him like the snow on his shoulders, but a hint of a smile settled into the corners of his hard mouth. He held out his gloved hands, moving his fingers. "Now your turn."

"See? They wriggle perfectly." She waved her fingers on her good hand. "Everything is fine. Now, if you'll excuse us, Marshal—"

"Gable. Elijah Gable, and I want to see you move your injured hand." He didn't budge, his big form blocking her from leaving. "Looks to me you have broken your arm, Miss…?"

"Miss Christina Eberlee, and since I have no funds for a doctor, no, nothing is broken. You let the thief get away with my reticule, remember?" she couldn't help teasing.

"So this is my fault?"

"Somewhat."

"Then I suspect I owe you an apology." He looked up at her through spiky black lashes. "I should have run faster."

"Exactly." Why were the corners of her mouth trying to smile? She'd lost everything that mattered the most to her—the keepsakes were all she had left of those she loved. And this man made her want to forget everything with one small hint of his grin. There were good men everywhere, she thought, and it was nice to have a pleasant encounter with a lawman for a change instead of fearing them.

"Here comes the ticket agent." The marshal's tone rang with reassurance. "You were injured on their property. They should provide a doctor."

"Really, I'm fine." And embarrassed by the attention. Heavens! She shook her head at the uniformed man coming toward her. People were still staring, and the waiting train blared its five-minute warning. "I just need to rest, is all. C'mon, Annabelle."

"I do think you need medical care, Christina," Annabelle said.

What she needed was her reticule. She wanted to hold her adoptive mother's broach in her hand and remember the compassionate woman. She wanted to gaze just once more at the image inside the locket, those small girls' faces frozen forever in time, a reminder of love and family, things she did not have now.

And hadn't had in years.

"I'm sure you are right," she told her friend as she rose from the bench. She ignored her wobbling knees and rubbed at the cut on her hand. Yes, it certainly was bleeding. Fortunately, not too badly. "If it continues to worsen, I'll have a doctor in Angel Falls look at it. I promise."

"I'm going to hold you to that." Annabelle looked as if she meant it.

Warmth filled Christina's lonely heart. It had been a long time since anyone had cared for her. What a good friend Annabelle was. Indeed.

"I'm the one who failed to run fast enough." The marshal offered her his arm—and what a strong, reliable arm it was. "The least I can do is to see you onto the train and make sure you're settled comfortably."

"No need." She studied him—his rough, mountain-tough looks took her breath away. "Thank you for your kindness."

"Just doing my duty." He jammed his hands into his coat pockets, making a powerful image beneath the fall of lamplight.

Snow swirled around her as she stepped into the bite of the storm. She glanced over her shoulder for one last look at the man. "Goodbye, Elijah Gable."

"Maybe not, Miss Eberlee." He tipped his hat, the low tones of his voice stolen as the wind howled around her.

She stumbled after Annabelle, trying not to remember her other less-than-kind encounters with lawmen over the past handful of years. The local sheriff arriving at the homestead to tell of her adoptive father's deadly fall from a horse. A year later his deputy knocking at the door with eviction papers. Local law enforcement hauling her from the back stall of a livery stable, where she'd curled up for a night's sleep. Being accused of stealing food from a grocer when her stomach audibly rumbled with hunger—which it wouldn't have done if she'd been the thief in question.

"Christina?" Annabelle's cultured voice cut into her thoughts. "Do you need help getting up the steps?"

"No. You've been so good to me. Thank you."

"It's what friends do for one another." Annabelle reassured her with a smile.

She climbed into the shelter of the train, shivering from cold and shock, and stumbled to her seat. Her stomach twisted up with a hint of nausea. Fine, perhaps it was time to admit at least to herself that her arm may be broken after all.

After Annabelle settled in next to the window, Christina collapsed beside her, grateful to close her eyes for a moment. She just had to hold on through the rest of the day's journey, and surely her husband-to-be would help her.

She tried to envision a caring man, gentle-voiced like her adoptive father had been, but her fears returned. She blinked hard, but the image of warts, a bald pate, a severe overbite and all that hair jumped into her mind's eye and refused to leave.

Lord, let Tom be as wonderful as his letter. Please. Prayer filled her heart, full of so many unspoken wishes for her life. She'd been wandering for so long, since her mother's death. The hardship of her mother's medical debts, the loss of her job and the economy had each been a blow.

She was weary of sleeping in stalls and stables, in back doorways and abandoned buildings, working for day wages in hot kitchens, endless fields or drafty hotels. Nothing had worked out and although her faith was strong, she had to wonder why the Lord had put these hardships in her life. Maybe this chance with Tom was a better path, the good future God meant for her. She surely hoped so.

All she really wanted for Christmas was a home, a place to belong.

So why did the marshal's face slip into her thoughts? Granite strength, chiseled cheekbones, steely jaw.

"Hello again, Miss Eberlee." A familiar voice sounded next to her ear. "How's that arm feeling?" Marshal Gable asked.

"A tad tender."

"I told the conductor what happened, how you fell on the railroad's property and convinced them they had an obligation for your care."

"Oh, I wish you hadn't." Pink crept across her face, making her even prettier, if that were possible.

"I brought you a poultice. One of the cooks in the dining car whipped it up for me. Said it would help with the bruising."

"That's very kind of you." Surprise flitted across her gentle features. "You went to too much trouble."

"Not at all, considering I failed at my professional duties," he quipped.

"You can't fool me. You're not responsible and you failed at nothing. You're just being nice."

"Force of habit."

"That I believe." She carefully pushed up her sleeve. "Tell me what a Montana marshal is doing on a train?"

"I delivered a wanted man to the proper authorities in Chicago."

"And you're on your way home?"

"Yes, but wherever I am, my sworn duty is the same. To serve and protect." Elijah leaned in to lay the warm, doubled-over cloth on her lean forearm. A terrible bruise discolored her ivory skin. His heart twisted painfully in sympathy—nothing more. No way a rough, tough lawman like him could be interested in a sweet dainty miss like her. No possible way. A combination like that only spelled trouble.

"My, it feels so much better." Her cornflower-blue gaze communicated her appreciation.

Looking into her honest eyes made his heart tug strangely. It surprised him, considering he'd closed up his heart to softer feelings long ago. He ought to stand up, head back down the aisle to his seat three cars down and forget about this young lady with her heart-shaped face, rich brown curls and compelling eyes. But did he?

No, he stayed where he was, blocking the aisle,

kneeling beside her. "I broke my arm a few years back. I was riding on regular patrol with two other marshals. One was a trainee, a real greenhorn, and I figured I'd give him a few tips. So there I was instructing him on the proper demeanor of a Montana Range Rider and my horse startled. He reared, tossed me in the air like I was a sack of potatoes and wham, I hit the ground."

"Pride goeth before a fall?"

"Something like that. I got up, dusted myself off and realized my hat brim was bent, I'd broken my arm and ripped out the back seam of my trousers. I was the laughingstock of the unit." He chuckled, remembering the humiliation. "It took years to live down, especially the trouser seam. I had to ride all the way to Cedar Peak with my union suit showing. Did I mention it was winter? It was snowing, and I was mighty chilly."

"You're making that up."

"It's the truth. God willing, I learned my lesson so that doesn't happen again. But seeing as I'm a man and prone to mistakes, it's anyone's guess how long it will be before my dignity takes a fall again."

"I'm beginning to think you aren't terribly good at your job, Marshal." Humor put little sparkles in her eyes and curved her rosebud mouth into the most amazing smile he'd ever seen. *Lovely* was too mild a word to describe her and *beautiful* too common. Miss Christina Eberlee was extraordinary. She tilted her head to one side, studying him intently. "First you can't catch the boy with my reticule and now you confess you can't stay on your horse."

"I appreciate you not mentioning the torn seam. The guys still tease me every now and then. The broken arm mended and I bought a new hat, but my pride has never been the same." His chuckle died away as a spark lit up his heart, giving light where there had only been darkness before.

All because of her smile.

"Miles City, next stop!" the conductor called from the end of the car.

"Miles City," Christina repeated, turning to her traveling companion and exchanging words he could not hear and didn't try to.

He couldn't say why he felt the way he did, unable to look away, noticing every little thing about her. The elegant curve of her slender shoulder, the graceful column of her neck and the curl of her dark eyelashes against her cheek. The spark in his heart continued to burn like a newly lit candle in the void that had become his heart.

He hadn't felt anything like this since his fiancée died well over a dozen years ago.

"Promise me you'll write." Christina's dulcet voice reached him as the train slowed with a squeal of brakes.

"Of course. Christina, we must stay friends." The other woman spoke as the car jerked to a stop. "This is such a fine adventure we are both on. You must write and tell me what Tom is like."

"And you must tell me about Adam." Christina stood and stepped out of the way so her friend could leave. "You've been a blessing to me on this trip, An-nabelle. Know I'm praying for your marriage. May it be filled with great happiness."

"I'll be praying for you, as well." Annabelle squeezed Christina's good hand before walking re-gally away, disappearing down the stairs.

They were all alone now. His pulse galloped as he debated taking the empty seat next to her and continu-ing their conversation. Maybe he'd buy her lunch be-cause she didn't have the funds for a meal, what with her reticule gone. That felt like his fault, too.

"I hope she gets every wonderful thing she de-serves." Christina slipped into her seat, taking care to readjust the poultice. With a flick of her gorgeous brown locks, she strained to look out the window, where the falling snow had ceased, giving way to gray skies. "Oh, look at those lovely children she gets to be a mother to. Like me, she's a mail-order bride."

"A *what?*" His pulse screeched to a stop. He couldn't have heard her right. "A mail-order *bride?*"

"I'm on my way to meet my husband-to-be." Chris-tina blew out a shaky breath, sounding a little appre-hensive, a little hopeful.

"Is that right?" His voice sounded tinny, even to his own ears. "You're getting married, huh?"

"That's why I'm on this train. I'm going home— to my new home. Someplace I belong and will never have to leave." Hope lit her up. "I'm hoping to marry on Christmas Eve day."

"Well, congratulations." Disappointment hit like

a blow. He swallowed hard. So, she was spoken for. "Best wishes."

"Thank you. It won't be long and I'll be meeting Tom for the first time."

"Tom." The man had a name. He fought to ignore the squeeze of pain in his chest where the light dimmed, sputtering like a candle burning out. "I pray he's a good husband to you. You deserve that."

"You're a kind man, Elijah. I'm glad we had this chance to meet."

"The pleasure has truly been mine." He tipped his hat, taking a step away. He didn't tell her that for twelve long years his heart had been as cold as stone, as dark as a starless night.

Until her.

He spotted a man with a medical bag making his way down the aisle. "Here's the doctor I asked the conductor to find. You take good care of yourself and that arm. Have a nice life now, you hear?"

"Yes, sir—Elijah." His name on her lips had never sounded so good. His heart lurched as he tipped his hat to her.

So, that was that. He'd learned the hard way years ago that love was all about timing. Once again, he'd felt the right things at the wrong time. As he headed to his seat, leaving Christina behind, the wintry chill in the air burrowed deep into him and would not leave.

Chapter Two

Angel Falls. Chilly air burned Christina's face as she stepped from the train onto the platform. Ice crunched beneath her shoes as she savored her first look at the town that was to become her home. Snow mantled the train station's roof and clung to evergreen boughs. It frosted the rooflines of a street of shops and a few small shanties across the way. A gray sky stretched overhead from horizon to horizon and the shining peaks of the distant Rocky Mountains rose up to disappear into the low clouds.

Home. The word filled her with possibilities. She gripped the red handle of her black satchel more tightly with her good hand, hardly aware of the hustle of folks climbing off the train behind her. She searched the small crowd for Tom's face. Let him not be too hairy, she hoped. Her palms felt damp against the wool of her green mittens as she waited for her husband-to-be to step forward and claim her.

This was what she'd prayed so hard for, day to day

and from night to night. All around her, families re-united or said farewells, clinging to one another, sharing loving looks. Husbands and wives, mothers and sons, friends and sisters. Gentle wishes and cries of welcome or sad sounds of parting peppered the air around her. A lovely family crowded together, re-united, a mom flanked by two beautiful little girls while her husband kissed each daughter on the cheek. Tears stood in their eyes. Anyone could see the love that bound them. The happiness they felt when they were together.

Please, let that be me one day. It was what she wished with all her heart.

"Ma'am?" A country-looking man in a brown hide coat swept off his wide-brimmed hat. His brown hair was a little too long and mussed, and his abundant facial hair all but hid his mouth and a good deal of his collar.

Maybe she could talk him into a trim, she thought optimistically, refusing to be disappointed. He looked less prosperous than she'd hoped with his threadbare trousers and patched boots, but his eyes were kind. That was a prayer come true. That was what mattered.

"Tom?" she asked excitedly, suddenly so nervous her mouth felt numb. "It's wonderful to meet you."

"Sorry, I ain't Tom." He put his hat back on, looking disappointed. "I'm Jed. Guess you ain't Aida, either."

"No, I'm sorry." She truly was. She watched as Jed continued down the length of the platform. Another woman stood at the far end, looking lonely. Christina wished she'd known there was another mail-order bride on the train. Her mind drifted to Annabelle. How were things going with her? Was Adam all she'd hoped for?

"Excuse me, miss?" A very proper-looking man in a black suit approached her. A top hat hid most of his sleek, well-combed black hair. This couldn't be Tom, since the man looked like a butler and not a farmer. "You wouldn't happen to be Miss Louisa Bell?"

"No, sorry." She watched as the man moved on, searching out the only other lone female waiting on the platform.

The rumble of the engine vibrated through the boards at her feet. The wind gusted, swirling her skirts around her ankles. She prayed no one could see the hole in her sock or the state of her well-mended shoes. She drew her brown coat more tightly around her, unsure what to do. There were no other single men on the platform. She'd been quite clear in her letter to Tom about the day and time she would be arriving. Perhaps something had held him up? Or, worse, perhaps the letter had been lost in transit?

A little of her happiness leaked out with her next breath. A flake of snow struck her cheek, and she shivered. The hustle of the crowd had gone.

"How's the arm?" The rumble of a smoky baritone drew her attention. Marshal Elijah Gable tipped his hat to her. "Still just bruised?"

"Yes, exactly, and feeling much better." Not that

she could move her fingers yet, but she was hopeful. "What are you doing loitering around the depot?"

"Oh, keeping my eye out for crime or nefarious-looking ruffians."

"So a big part of your job is just standing around doing nothing?"

"Something like that." Little did she know he'd been watching over her. "I also help damsels in distress."

"If I see any, I'll point them in your direction." Blue flecks in her eyes glittered up at him.

The stubborn light within him strengthened like an ember refusing to be put out. "This clearly isn't my business, but your fiancé hasn't shown up to claim you."

"He's coming, I'm sure." She glanced around the empty platform, maybe thinking she was hiding her anxiety. Behind them the train rumbled, like a giant beast ready to bolt. "Perhaps he got waylaid."

"Maybe." Elijah couldn't imagine anything that would cause him to leave Christina alone in a strange town and penniless. "Why don't I help you get settled, so you're not standing here all afternoon?"

"Oh, no. Tom said he'd meet me here, and that's right where I'll be when he comes." She motioned toward the cozy little station where lamplight shone through frosted windowpanes. "I will be warm and safe there, so go about your business. I see no damsels in distress here."

"That's too bad. Just thought you might want some company." Snowflakes drifted lazily on a gusting wind, harbingers of another storm coming. He planted a hand on his hat, holding it when a gust hit. "It might get cold waiting."

"I'm sure he won't be much longer." The dainty curve of her chin hiked up a notch. "Any number of things could have happened. A sick animal on his farm or a broken axle on the drive to town could have delayed him. There could have been an accident on one of the streets in town and he stopped to help. He's a reliable man, my Tom. He'll come."

"I'm sure. The thing is, the station closes between trains. There won't be another one until morning." As proof, the lamplight went out, leaving the small window in darkness. A tall, pole-skinny man opened the door and took out his keys to lock it behind him. "With the sun about to set, it might get cold waiting here."

"Yes, it might." She bit her bottom lip, studying one of the benches tucked up against the side of the station house. "I'm sure Tom won't be much longer."

Was she aware of the slight wobble in her voice, the one hinting that maybe she wasn't so sure?

This isn't your business, he tried to tell himself. Being near to her like this would only make him hurt more, because as she stood in the hazy light before sunset, dappled with snow and lovelier than anything he'd ever laid eyes on, he cared about her. He didn't know why she brought life to his heart. He only knew she did.

A cruel truth, because she was not free. He could only pray that the man who'd claimed her was worthy of her. A smart man would walk away. This was a safe town, he and his fellow lawmen worked to keep it that way, but no young woman should be sitting alone in the cold and dark. It was his professional duty to see her somewhere safe, and that made it a little easier to snatch the battered satchel from her gloved hand.

"Hey, that's mine." Soft tendrils of brown silk framed her heart-shaped face in airy little wisps. "You are helping me against my will, Marshal."

"Sorry, it's my sworn duty. The train is leaving—" He paused while the whistle blew loud and long. "Your Tom will know to look for you at the hotel. This isn't a big town. There aren't a lot of other places you could go."

"I don't know which hotel he made my reservation at." Her gait tapped alongside his, as lightly as a waltz. "I'm afraid we didn't exchange many letters."

"You were in a hurry to wed?"

"Very much so, as I was sneaking into the local livery stable to sleep during the night and creeping out before the owner arrived each morning." Her chin hiked another notch. "I could have been arrested for trespassing if I'd been caught. What do you think about that, Marshal?"

Her tone remained light and sweet, but it took a like soul to hear the hollowness beneath. He clomped down the depot steps.

"I do know how that feels." His honesty surprised him. His past wasn't something he dredged up. He followed the boardwalk, staying at her side. "My par-

ents lost our farm when I was ten. We lived out of
our wagon for two years. Pa would work wherever he
could find day wages, usually harvesting or planting.
In the heat of the summer or the bitterest days of winter I slept in the back of the wagon. Then one day, the
wagon broke down, Pa couldn't afford the repairs and
so we slept where we could."

"You were homeless, too?" Surprise softened her,
opened her up in a way he'd never seen in anyone before. She had a pure heart, he realized. No guise, no
facade, just honesty. "So you know what it's like?"

"To be so hungry your stomach feels ready to gnaw
its way out?" He nodded, hating to remember those
tough times.

Her curls bobbed as she nodded her head. Yes, she
knew exactly what he meant. He was afraid of that.
He blew out a breath, hating she'd known that exis-
tence. Considering the worn and patched state of her
clothes, maybe she was still living it.

"I pray those times are behind you." He pitched his
voice to be heard above the approaching rattle of a
teamster's wagon. "I'm glad you found Tom. Life has
to get better from here, right?"

"That's the idea." Snow breezed between them, as if
to divide them. As if heaven were reminding him she
was not his to care about. "Do you know Tom Rutger?"

"No, sorry. Moved here in September." The side-
walk came to an intersection and he stopped. Christmas was in the air. Somewhere, perhaps a street or two

over, bells chimed. Sounded like Reverend Hadly was out collecting coins for the orphanage again.

"So, you're new to town, too." The storm swirled around them with sudden vengeance, veiling the horses pulling vehicles down the street. The shops on the other side were merely glimpses of shape and color before the snowstorm swallowed them. "Where did you move here from?"

"Helena. I was headquartered there. When the office opened here, I jumped at the chance."

"You always wanted to live in Angel Falls?"

"No, I was looking for a change. My pa passed away a few years back. Thought it might be a good time to start somewhere new."

"I'm glad you did, or we never would have met." Her smile could make him forget to breathe. Unaware, she brushed snowflakes out of her eyes. She peered up at him, her face rosy from the cold, asking a deeper question. "Did your pa find a job in Helena? Is that when you were able to find a home?"

Strange how two very different people—she, a little dainty thing and he a tough, lone-wolf of a lawman understood one another. She truly understood what a home meant. "My father finally landed a steady job working on a big farm overseeing the wheat fields just out of town. He only worked nine months out of the year and things were lean, but it was just the two of us. It was the turning point for us."

"Just the two of you? What happened to your mother?"

"She passed away when I was eleven." Those were times he didn't talk about. He didn't explain there had been no money for a doctor, and the wagon had proved too cold a shelter in winter.

But Christina seemed to know that without him having to say so. Understanding shone in her eyes. "I'm so grateful you had your pa."

"We got through it together." He swallowed hard, grateful not to have to explain further. Strange how she could understand him like that. "The hotel is across the street. We'll get you checked in and I'll leave a note for Rutger at the train depot, so he knows where to find you, even though it's the only hotel in town."

"Thank you, Elijah." His name rolled off her tongue like a hymn, sweet and reverent, and the sound filled him up. He admired whoever Tom Rutger was for his choice in a bride. A smart man—one not pining after another's intended—ought to get moving and stop wishing. He took her elbow to help her across the street but a horse's shrill whinny of alarm stopped him.

He couldn't see much through the curtain of snow. Harnesses jangled. A lady screamed.

"Whoa!" a man called out as shadowy wagons skidded to a stop. Horses reared in alarm and a load of lumber crashed to the ground.

Elijah was running before he'd even realized he'd stepped off the boardwalk. His gaze riveted to a small form lying motionless in the middle of the chaos.

"He came out of nowhere, Marshal." The teamster jumped down from his wagon. Panic-stricken, the man dropped to his knees beside the still body. "He's just a little tyke. He ran in front of my horses. Couldn't stop 'em in time."

"Are you okay, boy?" Elijah brushed the muddy snow from the mired street off the boy's face. Lashes blinked up at him as the child tried to stir, but he slipped back into unconsciousness. Just a little guy, maybe eight years old. Somebody's son, somebody's loved one. He laid a hand on the boy's chest, relieved at the steady heartbeat.

"He's still breathing." Christina knelt beside him with a swish of her skirts. Distress wreathed her lovely face. She ran tender fingers across the child's forehead. "He has quite a bruise already, and a lump."

"My horse done it." The teamster's face twisted, torn up. "Must have hit him with a hoof when he reared up in surprise. Will he be all right?"

"Head injuries can be dangerous," Christina said, taking the end of her scarf and gently swiping the boy's face with her good hand. The child moaned, stirring again. "That's a good sign. How are you feeling, sweetheart?"

The boy's eyelids fluttered, but he didn't open them. Small, scrawny, scared, he was a ragamuffin who could use a good meal. Poor kid.

"Anyone know who he is?" Elijah asked.

"I don't, sorry, Marshal." The teamster shook his head.

"Never seen 'im before." Les from the lumberyard ambled over. "I saw the whole thing. The boy ran out of the mercantile like a rabbit being chased by a coyote. Didn't even stop to look for traffic."

"He darted into the road," agreed elderly Mrs. Thompson from inside her covered carriage. "I don't recognize him, and I know everybody in this town."

"Thanks, ma'am." He scooped up the boy carefully, cradling him in his arms. "Anyone else hurt?"

"Nope." The teamster's concern remained carved on his rugged face. "I'll check in with your office later. See how the boy's doing."

"I'd appreciate that." The weight of the boy in his arms reminded him of his new mission. The doc's office wasn't far. He turned to the woman at his side. "I guess this is where our paths part again."

"You're wrong about that." Her chin hiked up as she gripped her satchel's handle with her good hand and accompanied him around the maze of stopped vehicles. "I want to help you with that little boy."

"But what about your intended?" He stepped onto the boardwalk. "You might miss him."

"Tom and I will find each other. I believe that is God's will for us." It felt easy to think so in this small, cozy town graced with white. She loved the way snow made everything fresh and new. This is what she hoped to make of her life, to recover it and start again. Thanks to Tom, she had the chance to belong and find a real home, to have a husband and one day a family. Helping the wounded boy felt like her first act in this new life. *Do the right thing,* her adoptive mother used to say, and it will always work out right in the end. "Right now, this boy needs us."

"He does." Elijah led the way down the opposing street, walking with quick certainty. Masculinity radiated from him with quiet assuredness.

He seemed like a man comfortable with who he was, a man sure of what he stood for. Soft feelings rose within her, but that was only natural. It was impossible not to admire a man cradling an injured boy in his arms, keeping the child tucked safely to his chest for warmth.

Yes, simply a little admiration, that's all, she told herself, praying Tom would be like Elijah—good, decent, strong and caring. A man who would cradle their children in his arms one day.

"What is a child that age doing running around on his own?" she asked as they hurried down the boardwalk. "Why didn't his parents come running?"

"Good question. Maybe they are busy in one of the shops." He nodded in recognition of a man in a dark coat riding a fast-moving horse in the direction of the wagon accident. A star glinted on his chest. "There's the sheriff. He'd spot anyone searching for a missing child here in town and send them on to the clinic."

"Oh, the boy's waking up." Christina leaned in closer with her soft lavender fragrance and sweetness. Her gleaming hair held highlights of cinnamon in the late day's light. As the brim of her blue hat brushed his jaw, places long dark in his heart brightened.

He didn't feel the weight of the boy or the cold of

the wind or hear the clatter and chaos echoing down the street. All he could see was her. The cute slope of her nose, the big wide blue eyes focused on the child in his arms and her caring expression burnished her, making her more incredible than anything in their snowy surroundings.

"Hello, there." She smiled into unfocused, blinking eyes. "Do you remember what happened?"

The boy groaned in pain and rolled against Elijah's chest, burrowing closer as if to his parent. Perhaps the boy was confused. Not surprising he would be after being hit like that. Elijah ignored a stab of longing. The promise of a son had died with his fiancée long ago.

"What is your name?" she asked gently, not wanting to startle the child.

No answer. The boy took one look at her and hid his face against Elijah's jacket.

"That's quite a lump you have on your head." Her gentle attempt to talk to the boy garnered nothing. The child didn't move.

Was he crying? Or just trembling from the cold? Elijah couldn't tell. He glanced down the street, half expecting to see a worried mother dashing down the boardwalk after him. Nothing.

"Guess he doesn't want to talk to us," Elijah quipped. "Must be a good sign?"

"Must be. Does your head hurt?" she persisted.

Nothing. The boy was probably just scared, Elijah thought.

"You'll be all right," he reassured him. "We'll get

you looked at. Doc Frost's a nice doctor. He's got two girls about your age."

Still no response. The boy wasn't bleeding and he didn't seem badly hurt. All good things in his favor.

As Elijah glanced over his shoulder one more time, he spotted something else beyond the crowd of onlookers. A man strode across the street coming from the direction of the train depot. His jaw set, his posture stiff, his quick steps angrily stalking toward the hotel.

Tom Rutger? He winced, not wanting it to be so. The foreboding lodged in his chest told him otherwise. Christina's groom had come to claim her. The man stalked into the hotel and disappeared, but likely he'd reemerge in a minute or so. That was all the time he had left with Christina.

"Maybe this is where we go our separate ways." He stopped in front of the clinic door. "Go on back to the hotel."

"But I want to stay until his parents come." Torn, she set down her satchel and ran her fingertips across the boy's head. The child wouldn't look at either of them, stiff with tension.

"He needs a doctor now." He clutched the child to him, taking a step back. "I can manage it from here."

"But I feel as if I should do more."

"I know, but the child is my duty now. Look, your Tom is coming."

"You'll let me know what happens, right? I'll be at the hotel. You could drop by and tell me his parents found him." She scooped up her satchel. "I want to make sure his story gets a happy ending, too."

A happy ending sounded nice, but stopping by to see her? Not a good idea. He opened the door instead of answering her. He would make no promises he didn't intend to keep. Heat from the potbellied stove inside the clinic washed over him, but he shivered as if with cold. Probably it had to do with the brawny, blond-headed man storming up the boardwalk behind Christina. Dark eyes bored into his. No way to miss the clear message of possession.

"Thanks for your assistance, Miss Eberlee." Elijah nodded in farewell, reined in his feelings and stepped into the clinic. The boy sniffed against his chest, clinging hard. Probably worried about what his ma would say once she caught up to him. "Goodbye."

"Goodbye." The last daylight vanished, the colors and light of the world bled away and stole his last view of her. The brightness in his heart turned to black as he let the door swoosh shut behind him and handed the boy over to the doc.

Chapter Three

"Christina?" The voice behind her rumbled in a cool tenor. "Brown coat, blue hat, green mittens. Carrying a black satchel with a red handle. Just like your letter promised."

"Tom." Breathless, she spun to face him. Anticipation pounded through her like merry jingle bells. This was her husband-to-be. The man she would spend the rest of her days with, the man who would be her everything.

The last dregs of twilight made it hard to see him. He stood before her in shadow. His beefy shoulders spoke of strength and capability. The outline of his Stetson hinted at a hardworking man who spent his time in the Montana sun.

"It's so nice to meet you," she breathed, charmed when he swept her satchel from the boardwalk for her. "I had meant to wait at the depot for you, but the marshal said it would be cold and dark, as there were no more trains expected."

"I was a mite disappointed to find no one there." He had a pleasant voice with a vulnerable sound to it, as if he harbored great feeling deep beneath his rough exterior.

A wedge of lamplight reflected when a shop's door opened, giving her a brief glimpse of his jawline—hairless. At least she didn't have to worry about a foot-long beard. Definitely a good sign.

"I was on my way to the hotel when a boy was struck by a startled horse," she explained.

"I figured the hotel might be where you was headed." Instead of backtracking, Tom stepped toward her and kept on going. "Sorry to say, you won't be stayin' there. I got ya a place at the boardinghouse."

"Oh, I didn't know." She stopped herself from wondering about Elijah. It was the boy who troubled her, who'd burrowed into the marshal's coat like a baby bunny caught in a snare. He'd looked trapped, defeated. Determined to check on him as soon as she could, she tucked her aching arm against her side and followed Tom down the snowy boardwalk. "You and I didn't have much time to exchange letters, with your proposal and train ticket arriving the way it did."

"I didn't dare risk waiting too long. I knew a lady like you had options. I didn't want to lose out, not again." Sadness ticked across his shadowed face and weighed down his voice.

"What do you mean, again?"

"I've been lookin' for a wife for some time. In fact, you're the third lady I've proposed to this year." He offered his gloved hand to help her off the boardwalk and onto the street.

Her heart didn't leap at their first touch. Her soul didn't whisper to her, *he's the one*, as she'd hoped. But she also knew it would be improbable that she and Tom would be a match at first. Love took time and nurturing. But she wanted to love him. It was enough that he stayed beside her, protecting her from the brunt of the wind the way a true gentleman would.

"I took too much time thinking things over with those other ladies," he explained. "By the time I got around to writing, first one and then the other had already been claimed. With you I wrote right away. You were too much to miss out on."

That touched her. Her heart gave a little sigh. She wanted to be wanted. She wanted to matter to someone. She held tightly to his hand as she swept up onto the boardwalk. Light spilled over them, showing him fully for the first time.

Rustic. His fur coat made him look like a bear. His wide-brimmed hat hid most of his round face. He'd never be called handsome with his rather large nose and prominent chin, but his eyes were a friendly hazel and his muscular shoulders gave him a strong and dependable air. Looks weren't what mattered. Neither did riches. It was the man within that counted.

"This ain't the best place in town, but it's what I can afford." Tom shrugged in apology. "It's safe and warm, and I talked to the manager, who promised to make you welcome."

"Thank you, Tom." His thoughtfulness did more to reassure her than anything could. Snow brushed her cheek as she stepped past the door he held open for her. She caught a glimpse of denim trousers and boots as she swept into the light and warmth. "You've done so much for me. Sending me a train ticket, offering me your home and your love. I hope we can be happy together."

"You'll make me very happy indeed." He looked her up and down. Something glittered in his gaze, something she didn't understand, but it was gone before she could analyze it.

Perhaps it was simply the reflection of the lamplight in his eyes, she decided. He stood, perfectly valiant, swept off his hat and self-consciously ran his fingers through his dark blond hair. She felt self-conscious, too, worrying he would be disappointed in her, perhaps wishing she was prettier and trying to ignore the niggle of what felt like doubt in the pit of her stomach.

That's not a sign, she told herself. Anyone would feel trepidation meeting the stranger she'd agreed to marry. She'd prayed hard on this. Hadn't she felt peace in her soul after discussing this with God? And it wasn't as if she had a better choice. She'd answered twenty advertisements men had placed looking for wives in the *Hearts and Hands* magazine. Tom had been the one to answer her with a proposal and a train ticket. To a homeless woman, he'd been an answered prayer.

That's what he still was. The answer to her prayers. She watched as he spoke respectfully with the middle-aged woman behind the front desk. He unbuttoned his coat, showing a wedge of flannel shirt and red suspenders. Her husband-to-be was apparently a farmer, which would make her a farmer's wife. She knew nothing about farming, but she vowed to work hard. She would do her best cooking for him and keeping house. She'd learn about chickens and pigs or whatever she needed to because this man was going to be her everything. This man had promised to give her a home, his home, for Christmas.

"Mildred will get you settled." Tom thrust out the battered satchel. "I'll come by tomorrow right after lunch. Say, one o'clock?"

"I'll be ready." Christina took her satchel and tried to ignore the hollow feeling settling into the pit of her stomach. "I'm looking forward to it. I can't wait to see your farm."

"Can't wait to show it to you." Tom gave a bashful smile. "Good evening, Christina."

Her throat closed up watching him go. He donned his hat, straightened his bulky fur coat and pushed through the door with a powerful snap. An icy wind blew snow around him and he disappeared into the night and storm.

"C'mon, dearie." Mildred shuffled from behind the desk, heading toward the stairs. "I got your room a-warmin'. It's gonna be a cold one tonight."

"That's kind of you." What was she doing feeling

lonely? Perhaps disappointed? Tom likely had chores to do on his farm instead of spending time getting to know her over supper, which she hadn't realized until now that she'd been hoping he would.

There is plenty of time for that, a lifetime, she told herself as she followed Mildred not up the staircase but down a set of narrow steps into the basement. In a few days she would be fixing supper in their home. There would be endless evenings ahead to ask questions about his childhood or to tell him of hers. It will work out, she thought optimistically. It had to.

"Here ya go." Mildred opened a door. "Coffee and tea are complimentary, self-serve if you're interested. Let me know if you'll be taking supper as Mr. Rutger didn't pay for your meals, only your room. It's fifty cents, a real bargain."

Fifty cents? Christina bowed her head to hide her disappointment. She thought of her lost reticule, ignored her growling stomach and tightened her grip on her satchel. "Not tonight, thank you."

"All righty." Mildred gave a motherly smile. "The coal hod is stocked. Come find me if you need anything, dearie."

"I will." Christina waited until the older woman left before squeezing through the narrow door. The small room was cozy with a comfortable bed, a darling bureau and two armchairs, a peephole window and coal heater in the corner. Better than she'd had in years.

She tucked her satchel next to the bureau, sat on the foot of the bed and rested her aching arm.

I'm not disappointed, she thought stubbornly, willing it to be so.

"Doc, do you know much about a man named Tom Rutger?" Elijah held out the basin of warm wash water he'd poured and carried from the woodstove.

"Tom? Sure I know him. I know just about everyone in this county." Sam Frost took the basin, dunked a washcloth into the sudsy water and returned to his little patient's side. "Why are you asking? Is it official business?"

"No, just curious is all." He glanced toward the dark window, remembering the brief outline of the man who Christina was going to marry . "I didn't like the look of him."

"He and his brother took over the family pig farm when their folks retired, oh, seven or eight years ago. The brother married and moved onto his wife's place last summer." Doc Frost swiped at the mud obscuring the injured boy's face.

No worried mother had knocked at the door looking for her child. No father had frantically searched the streets for a son that had wandered off. Elijah stared beyond his reflection in the window and studied the dark boardwalk. No one would be coming for the boy. He felt it in his guts. Returning his thoughts to the subject of Tom Rutger, he said, "I think I know which farm you mean. Just east of town?"

"That's the one."

Elijah leaned his forehead against the cool glass, picturing the run-down barn, the pig shelters made of scrap lumber, the shanty that had never seen a coat of paint. Tom Rutger might be the far side of prosperous, but that hadn't answered the question. "Is he a good man?"

"I don't like to talk ill of others. Let that be enough said." Sam let out a sigh.

"That's what I was afraid of." He couldn't stop wondering about Christina. Where was she now? Maybe dining with her bridegroom? They'd walked down the boardwalk away from both the hotel and other eating establishments in town, save for the boardinghouse.

He wished he could get the black feeling out of his stomach. With a sigh, he searched the stormy street. He did spot someone else he knew on the boardwalk. Sheriff Clint Kramer lifted a hand in acknowledgment and moseyed over.

"There's the sheriff. Maybe he has some news on the boy." Elijah headed for the door.

"Good. I'll get him cleaned up." Sam rinsed out the cloth. "Maybe while you're gone, I can get him to talk."

"That would be an improvement." Elijah donned his hat, burst onto the boardwalk and his boots took him straight to the sheriff.

"No one is looking for the boy . As far as I can tell, no one knows who he is," Clint said, jabbing his hands into his coat pockets. "Angel Falls is a small enough town—someone ought to know him."

"So where does that leave us?" He couldn't abandon the boy. Hard to forget how the kid had sobbed, face pressed against Elijah's chest. "Maybe the doc can keep him at the clinic overnight?"

"That'd be best. I'll leave a note on the office door, in case his parents decide to come looking for him." Clint tipped his hat, taking a step back. "Talk to you later, Elijah."

"Later." Snow bit his cheeks and swirled in a furious dance down the dark, empty street. His thoughts should have stayed on the kid, but his gaze wandered to where lit windows in the boardinghouse glowed faintly through the storm.

Christina's angelic face filled his mind. Remembering her light chestnut locks and her willowy grace, the light she brought to his battered heart returned.

She's not yours, he reminded himself. If only that could keep his soul from wishing.

He stomped the snow from his boots and yanked open the clinic door. "Doc? Want me to grab some supper?"

"That's a fine idea." The doctor toweled off the boy's face with a practiced hand. "Since I've got a patient for the night, we'd best feed him. I'll send word to my nurse. She'll be the one staying with him, once I get settled."

"Sounds good." Elijah leaned against the door frame, studying the boy who lay as stiff as a board, staring hollowly at the wall. "Too bad the kid isn't talking. Yep, it's a shame. I won't be able to know what he wants for supper. Should I get him liver and onions? Boiled pig's feet soup? Or a tripe sandwich, maybe?"

"Order him the soup." Sam winked. "There's nothing more appetizing than seeing a swine hoof in your soup bowl."

"True enough." Elijah winked back, but the boy didn't stir. Hard not to notice the ragged clothes, or a string holding the leather toe to the sole of one shoe. A suspicion about the child lodged between Elijah's ribs, making it hard to breathe as he pushed away from the door. "I'll be back, Doc, with that soup and maybe a tripe sandwich or two."

"We'll be waiting," Sam assured him, fetching clean long johns out of a nearby drawer, which looked as if they might fit the boy.

The kid was too little to be on his own, Elijah thought to himself as he left the warmth and light for the dark and storm. Icy wind needled through his clothes as he faced into the wind. He met no one as he hurried down the snowy boardwalk, past businesses closed for the night and into the light shining from the boardinghouse.

He walked past a long row of windows, blazing brightly. A potbellied stove glowed red-hot in the room where a dozen tables lined the walls, filled with diners. Mildred spotted him through the window and waved, signaling him to hurry on in.

"There you are." Her smile put pink into her appled

cheeks. "I wondered where you got to. It's roast beef tonight, your favorite. I talked the cook into making those mashed potatoes you like."

"Mildred, you are a treasure, but I'm sort of still on duty." He thought of the homeless boy, rigid with fear. He knew what that was like. Long-ago memories threatened to whisper to the surface but he clamped them down in time. "Could you wrap up—"

That's as far as he got. Words failed him when Christina Eberlee waltzed from a shadowed stairwell and into sight. Her lustrous brown hair held highlights of nutmeg that gleamed like the finest silk in the candlelight and framed her ivory face to perfection. "You." Surprise crinkled her soft forehead. "What do I have to do to get rid of you, Marshal?"

"Don't know, ma'am. Perhaps take a flyswatter to me?"

"I'll keep it in mind for next time." Humor crooked her lush mouth upward. Her blue skirts swished around her ankles as she came to a stop in front of the tea service, halfway across the lobby. Without the bulk of the coat he'd always seen her in before, she looked even tinier. Slender, petite, as delicate as china.

He towered over her like Goliath. "I thought you were staying at the hotel."

"Change of plans." Her smile didn't dim. "What's your excuse?"

"I live on the top floor, for now, but I've been looking to buy a house." He swept off his hat, realizing too late he'd left it on too long. A gentleman would have taken it off sooner.

"Miss Eberlee, you know our illustrious marshal?" Mildred waved the younger woman over. "Why didn't you say so?"

"I didn't know he lived here." Christina waltzed over. "Buying a house sounds like a big step."

"I'm ready to settle down, plus this town feels like home." He wanted her to know she'd come to a good place. He hoped she liked Angel Falls as much as he did. "Folks are friendly, going to church is like being with family and this piece of Montana is beautiful. Can't go wrong by living here."

"See? That's another good sign from our Lord. I've been doing a lot of praying lately. Some days it's tough to have faith that hard times will turn into good." She drew in a little breath, as if grasping on to determination. "It really has to be changing for the better."

"That's my wish for you." He knew that when he knelt to say his prayers tonight, they would be for her.

"How is the boy?" she asked. "With his parents by now?"

"No one's come for him, and he's not talking." Elijah's jaw tightened at the sad situation.

"Why don't I show you to a table, just the two of you?" Mildred offered, charging toward the open dining room doors. "You can keep chatting while I fetch your meals."

"Oh, no." Christina took a step back. "I only came up for tea."

"No supper? But you must eat, dearie." Mildred looked stricken. "The kitchen closes in an hour. We don't stay open later like the hotel."

"I have a better idea," Elijah said. It was easy to see the problem. He guessed that Christina didn't have any money for supper. "Mildred, wrap up four roast beef suppers and a jug of hot tea. Doc has a patient staying at the clinic, and Christina is going to join us."

"I am?"

He wanted to do this the right way, so she wouldn't feel awkward about eating with them. "Neither Doc or I can get the kid talking. Maybe he'll open up to you where he doesn't trust us. Think of the meal as payment for your help."

"Oh." Her forehead crinkled as she considered his offer. "Fine, although I'm not sure it will be a fair bargain."

"True. Doc and I are getting the better part of the deal."

"You are a charmer. I'm going to have to keep my eye on you, Marshal." She looked up at him through dark lashes and his heart tumbled.

A harmless tumble, he told himself. Being sweet on a lady was no crime as long as he didn't wish for more.

"That's me, a real charmer. I haven't beaued a lady since I was twenty." His throat worked—even after a dozen years the loss hurt. It had become vague, it had become distant but Darcy had been his first love. As it turned out, his only chance for love and a family.

"Trust me, I'm so far out of practice I'm no threat to the lovely ladies of Angel Falls."

"I wouldn't say that was true." She sparkled up at him, her kindness capturing him. As if he wasn't caught enough.

"Four meals, ready to go." Mildred barreled in with the packages wrapped in thick paper. "And a crock of hot tea. You bring back the dishes, Marshal. I've got my eye on you."

"I'll toe the line, ma'am." He winked at the older lady, grateful for her intrusion. When it came to Christina, he'd be wise to keep his heart closed or she would surely break it.

Remembering what the doc had said about Christina's intended groom, he prayed that the pig farmer would fall hard for her, too, and be the good husband she deserved.

Love could make a man better, Elijah thought as he waited for Christina to fetch her coat from her room. *Lord, let that be true for Tom Rutger.*

Chapter Four

"Hello, there." Christina peeked around the door frame into the boy's room. The meal she carried, still steaming hot, made her stomach twist painfully in hunger. She breathed in the spicy richness of peppered roast beef, buttery mashed potatoes, doughy buttermilk biscuits and bacon-studded green beans. "The marshal thought you would like something to eat."

The child sat with his back to her and said nothing, staring at the wall. His slight shoulders drooped, his spine slumped and his mop of freshly washed hair promised to be a mix of blond and brown when it dried.

No one had come for him. Didn't anyone care?

"How does your head feel?" She set the plate on his bedside table.

No answer. His back rose and fell slightly with each breath.

"It's good to see that you're all right. I was really worried about you." She withdrew a napkin, which

Mildred had provided, from her skirt pocket and tucked it beside the plate. "I'm Christina. What's your name?"

The boy shook his head.

At least he'd acknowledged her. That was progress, right? Encouraged, she sat on the foot of the bed.

"I'm new to town. I only know the marshal, and now the doc and the lady who runs the boarding-house where I'm staying," she explained. "I could use a friend."

"Why?" One thin shoulder shrugged. "You're better off on your own."

"I've never found that to be true." She knew what it was like to feel alone and disheartened. "Friends always make life better. They help you, you help them. They share their life, you share yours. Why, I was all alone coming out here on the train—"

"The train?" he interrupted, his back stiffening rod-straight.

"—and I met someone who was feeling the same way," she continued. Maybe the boy had learned not to trust other people. Was there maybe a way he might open up to her? "Annabelle and I started talking and next thing you know, we were friends. Just like that, wanting to help each other and cheering each other on. I was hoping you would be my friend, too."

"Uh—" His emerald-green eyes stared up at her like a deer caught in a hunter's snare.

"I used to live in Dove's Way, Dakota Territory with my Ma and Pa, until Pa's death. Then Ma passed away late in the summer." She slipped the plate off the night table and held it out to him. "That's when I went to Spring Glen to look for work. It was a bigger town along the railroad. Where do you live?"

The boy gulped, still staring at her. His face turned red and he bowed his head. He took the plate from her and stared at it hungrily.

"I spotted a school bell tower when I was walking here." She heard footsteps in the hallway, coming closer. "I could see it over the tops of the buildings on the street. Is that where you go to school?"

Instead of answering, he seized the fork tucked on his plate and shoveled in a heap of mashed potatoes.

"Hey, good progress." Elijah shouldered into the room, seeming to fill it. She couldn't look anywhere but at him and his wind-tousled dark hair, his easygoing grin and strong, reassuring presence. He paced deeper into the room holding two plates of food. "You got him eating. Any chance he told you his name?"

"No, but he's going to have to, as we're now friends."

"Is that so?" Elijah set one plate on the nightstand. "Slow down there, fella. Eating so fast isn't good for you. I ought to know."

The boy didn't look up. He didn't slow down. A fringe of too-long hair tumbled over his forehead and hid his eyes as he forked in load after load. If he had glanced at the man before him, he would have witnessed the solemn understanding deep in the marshal's midnight-blue eyes. Maybe then the child wouldn't be so afraid.

"Still not using your left arm?" Elijah handed her a plate loaded with food.

"I'm just resting it. It's fine, really."

"Right. Like I believe that." He shook his head, scattering thick dark hair, and gave her a glimpse of a slight set of dimples. "You know I have plans for you and the doctor."

"I figured there was a price to be paid for this meal." She still couldn't wiggle her fingers, so maybe a doctor was needed. She set the plate on her lap, grateful for it. "Let's say grace."

"Sounds good to me." Elijah took her hand warmly in his own.

Little snaps of awareness skidded down her arm, heading straight for her soul. No need to worry about those little snaps. It was harmless, perhaps because she and Elijah were so alike. Without words they recognized the silent boy's plight because they had been there. Elijah's dark blue eyes riveted to hers, and the steady light of reassurance she read there drove out everything else.

Yes, his friendship was a surprise blessing. Proof that the good Lord watched over her every step of the way. In gratitude, she bowed her head. Before she closed her eyes she saw Elijah's broad, capable hand gently catch hold of the boy's. His fork stilled and he gave one last swallow.

"Thank you, Father, for the bounty of this meal. We are truly grateful." Elijah's deep tone rumbled like a hymn, reverent and earnest. "We are also thankful for the blessing of friends You have placed in our lives. Please let us find ways to help each other according to Your word. Amen."

"Amen." When she opened her eyes, the lamplight flickered more brightly and Elijah seemed to be surrounded with it, bronzed by the golden glow. His goodness shone through. She could see it clearly.

There is so much good inside of everyone, she reminded herself, thinking of Tom. Sometimes it just takes a while to get to know someone before you can see it. She needed to have faith. Tom had been the only man to answer her letter. She'd answered twenty advertisements that frigid November day when a magazine skidded down the alley she was huddled in, blowing like a leaf in the wind, and came to a stop at her feet. It was all the change she had for postage and paper. And it had led her here, where she was safe and warm with friends. She had to believe that God had brought her here for a reason.

"My ma taught me to pray." The boy's words came raspy, almost like a whisper. His bottom lip trembled as if using all of his courage. "Did your ma teach you?"

"She did." Elijah's answer rippled softly, warm and comfortable. His earnest wish to help the boy touched her. They'd left so much unspoken about the child. The ragged clothes, being too skinny and the haunted look in his wary green eyes all pointed to one simple truth.

"My older sisters showed me how to steeple my hands and kneel before my bed to pray at night." Christina found herself answering, longing for what was lost. She plopped a forkful of potatoes on her tongue, so good, so smooth and buttery. That's when she noticed the boy's plate was empty. She chewed and swallowed, planning on giving the boy half her food.

"My ma taught me, too." Elijah leaned over and slid half his roast beef slices onto the boy's plate. "She could sing like an angel. She was always humming one hymn or another, especially this time of year."

"We celebrated with music, too." Christina slid her biscuits onto the child's plate. "We would spend Christmas Eve going through all the carols and hymns we knew, singing along while my adoptive ma accompanied us on her piano."

"Did you ever learn to play?" Elijah's gaze met hers as he slid half of his potatoes from his plate to the child's.

"Yes." The memories warmed her and made what was lost closer. "I'm not nearly as good, but I can pound out a decent hymn or two."

"Decent?" He wasn't fooled. "Something tells me you can play better than that."

"I'll never tell." Merry chips of periwinkle twinkled in eyes as sweet as blueberries.

"How is our patient doing?" Doc Frost burst into the room. Elijah had been so absorbed, he hadn't heard a single footstep approaching. Absorbed by Christina's beauty, as any man in his right mind would be.

"His appetite is just fine," she quipped. In the soft light, her gentle nature shone through. Her rosebud mouth, perfectly made for smiling, curved upward in the corners like a cupid's bow. "Okay, I really am curious about your name. Just your first one. I can trade my green beans for it."

"Green beans?" the boy said. Her joke almost made him smile. "That's not a very good trade."

Her chuckle was like a chime of carillon bells. "Well, I suppose I could give you my dessert."

"There's dessert?" The boy's eyebrows shot up and he crammed a too-big piece of roast into his mouth.

"Chocolate cake." Christina cut a small bite of roast with the side of her fork. "With chocolate icing."

"It's a deal." The boy swallowed and sat back against the wall. The desperate look around his eyes faded, as he was no longer quite as hungry. "I'm Toby."

"It's nice to meet you, Toby," she said.

"Well, Toby, if you don't mind—" the doctor gestured toward Christina "—I'm going to borrow your new friend for a few minutes. But I promise you, the marshal will see to the doling out of dessert."

"I excel at that," Elijah quipped, sending the doc a grateful nod. "I'm a scrupulous lawman except for when it comes to chocolate cake. I just thought I should give fair warning."

"You wouldn't try to keep a slice for yourself, would you?" Christina rose gracefully, bringing her plate with her.

"Me? No way. I'd never do anything like that. Never." He winked, like a man feigning to do otherwise.

"I'll have you know, I'm immune to those dimples of yours." She swept away from him, unaware that he couldn't take his gaze from her. "Any woman would be mesmerized by them, but not me. So there's no need to go flashing them."

"I'll keep that in mind." He watched her leave the room with a swirl of her skirts. Down the hallway, over the pad of her step, she spoke to the doctor.

"I'll find a way to pay you, Doc, I promise you." Her quiet promise brooked no doubt. "Maybe I could clean your office in trade?"

"I'm sure we can work something out," the doctor answered, their voices fading to silence.

"She's really nice." Toby stuffed a biscuit into his mouth. "She'd make a real good ma."

"I'm sure she would." A little arrow of pain speared him. Best not to think about Christina as a mother or as Tom Rutger's wife. "It's time you and I had a little talk."

"Are you g-gonna arrest me?" Big green eyes widened. Toby glanced from window to door, like a trapped animal ready to bolt. "I didn't mean it, honest. I wished after I'd done it that I could take it back."

"You didn't mean to startle the horses." Elijah focused his attention on the kid. Toby shook his head, as if that wasn't what he'd meant to say. Curious about that, Elijah continued on. "No one else was hurt…no harm was done except for the teamster who had to restack his load."

"Oh. I'm real sorry about that, too. So, you ain't gonna throw me in jail?"

It was tough to gaze into those worried green eyes

and not feel something. It had to be hard being all alone. Elijah couldn't help caring. "Want to tell me what happened to your folks?"

"Uh—" Toby focused on the door. He jabbed another hunk of biscuit into his mouth, making it impossible to talk.

"Let me guess. They passed away." Elijah cut another bite of roast. "Was it very long ago?"

"Last year." Still chewing, Toby hung his head. "We all got sick, Ma, Pa, me and my little brother. I was the only one to get better."

"You don't have anyone looking after you?"

"Nope." He speared the last slice of beef on his plate. "After I ran off from the orphanage, I been doin' okay on my own."

"Let me guess. You rode in on one of the trains?"

"I've been riding the rails since summer." Toby set his fork on his empty plate. "I haven't got caught before. I run real fast."

"Want to tell me why you were running out of the mercantile?"

"No." Misery hung on him.

Not hard to figure what was going on. He'd have to talk to Lawson over at the mercantile next. "Toby, we're gonna have you stay the night here, where the doc's nurse can take care of you. Come morning, we'll get you a fine breakfast and talk some more. Is that okay with you?"

"Talkin' won't do no good."

"Just goes to show you've never talked much with

me before." He took Toby's empty plate and stood. "I'll go fetch your two pieces of cake from the other room. You know you're safe here, right, Toby?"

"I guess." He blew out a sigh. A line of tension remained burrowed into his forehead.

"Nothing bad will happen to you here. You have my word." Elijah paused in the doorway. "So sit tight until I come back. Do I have your word on that?"

Toby nodded. "Mister?"

"You can call me Elijah."

"You ain't gonna send me back to the orphanage, are you?" The kid's voice wobbled with worry.

"Not tonight. Your head has to hurt, so we'll talk about all that tomorrow. Tonight, you'll be safe and warm. I promise."

The boy nodded, as if in agreement. Elijah wasn't sure he could trust him. Best to speak with the nurse and make sure she kept a sharp eye on the door, just in case. Wind gusted against the siding as he left the room, a reminder of the frigid conditions outside. There was something about the kid. He'd come across runaways in his job before, but this one affected him.

He followed the sound of Christina's dulcet alto. "…I really had hoped it was just a bad bruise," she explained to the doctor. "Guess I was wrong."

"You'll need to keep icing it on and off to get the swelling down." The doc tucked a final piece of gauze into place and stood. "There. When you take her home, Elijah, make sure and get her ice from the kitchen."

"I'm perfectly capable of getting my own ice," Christina said, rolling her eyes.

"I'll take care of it." Elijah leaned one shoulder against the door. The sight of her filled him with peace. It took every scrap of his willpower to keep from tracing the curve of her cheek and the adorable tip of her chin with his gaze. *Stay unaffected, Gable,* he thought, straightening his spine. "So, it was broken. I was right all along?"

"Yes, yes, no need to comment on it."

He intended to say something light and breezy in return, but a loud *whap, whap, whap* echoed down the hallway behind him.

He stepped into Toby's room to find the window open and the shutter slapping the siding. No sign of the boy. His clothes and coat were missing from the closet. He really hadn't thought the boy would escape and leave chocolate cake behind.

Elijah hung his head. That was one dangerously cold winter storm and Toby was out in it. Alone.

"Elijah." Christina spotted the marshal in the small crowd of the late-breakfast rush at the boardinghouse. The red-hot stove struggled to heat the dining room. The morning might be cold, but the storm had blown out. A small blessing. "Elijah."

"Christina." The broad-shouldered marshal turned in his chair, and the smile that stretched his granite face when he spotted her drove the chill from the air.

"How's your arm feeling?" He bounded to his feet,

looking strappingly handsome in a dark shirt and denims. Likely every woman in the room swooned at the sight, and it wasn't only her.

"It's better. See, I can wiggle my fingers. The swelling is going down. The doc is going to be happy, since now he can splint it properly." She fiddled with her unbuttoned sleeve cuff, showing the makeshift splint over her broken wrist. "I can tell by looking at you that you didn't find Toby. I worried about him all night."

"Me, too." Shadows darkened his eyes. "I looked everywhere I could think."

"How late did you search?"

"No idea." He pulled out a chair at his table. "The storm finally turned bad enough that I had to stop."

"He's a smart boy." Christina couldn't ignore the fact that Toby knew how to get by. He'd been on his own for a good while. "He would know to find shelter and warmth."

"He was safe and warm where he was." Elijah's face compressed, a hint of his inner regrets. "I should have kept a better eye on him."

"I should have, too." She laid her hand on his, which rested on the back of the chair he held out for her. An act of friendship, that was all, a gesture of comfort. So why did it feel like more? Touching him was like coming home to a warm fire after being out in winter's cold. She removed her hand and settled into the chair he held for her, troubled by her reaction to him.

Maybe it was because she'd been alone, that's all. Of course it felt nice having friends again. First Annabelle and now Elijah. Tears of gratitude burned behind her eyes, even as she felt sad for Toby. Her life was changing for the better. She had friends, and in Tom she would have a husband and a home. The chance for a family and a happily-ever-after. She wanted that for the homeless little boy, too.

"Here, you may as well finish up the bacon." Elijah shoved a small plate in her direction.

"Oh, no, I just came in for tea."

"Fine, but I ordered too much. I'd hate to see it go to waste." He shrugged, as if it didn't matter to him, but it did. He turned over the clean cup at her place setting and lifted the small teapot sitting in the center of the table. "I was about to head out and continue my search for Toby."

"Judging by the way you're dressed, it's your day off." She studied the offered plate but didn't move to take it.

"Yes, I had time off for the holidays, so I may as well use it for Toby. I don't have much else to do but stay in and read." He poured himself a steaming cup of tea, too.

"You read? Me, too. At least when my ma was alive, if we weren't sewing or knitting, we were reading. Staying up way too late at night because we couldn't put our books down and come morning, we talked books over the breakfast dishes."

"You had a happy home."

"I did. The Lord was watching over me for sure when Ma and Pa came to choose a child." She looked wistful instead of sad, as if hoping the past could come around again. "I had it once, and it's what I'm wishing for again."

"I've noticed that you make your own happiness, Christina Eberlee." He liked that about her. He wished he could get past the knot of worry in his gut.

Please let Tom Rutger be good to her, he prayed. He wanted the man to do his best for her. She deserved that and more.

"So, what do you like to read?" she asked after bowing her head for a brief, silent grace. "Adventure novels?"

"Good guess. I can't put them down." He nudged the sugar bowl in her direction. "I was going to start *The Last of the Mohicans* last night, but—"

"But you were out looking for Toby." She stirred sugar into her tea. "I could hardly sleep last night thinking about him out in the cold."

"Me, either. I've already put in some time trying to track him down. Will do more when I leave here. We'll see if I can't bring in the little renegade."

"He's far too young to be on his own. You know he's been that way for a while. His clothes, his hair. How skinny he is." She thought of the past five months spent sleeping in the shelter of alleys or stables. Toby deserved better. "And what about the bruise on his head?"

"The doc said he looked fine—it was just a hard bump, but he needs to be looked after. I'll find him... don't worry. I won't stop until I do."

"What will happen to him then?" She already knew the answer, her stomach knotting as she took a bit of bacon.

"The orphanage." Elijah shrugged, a helpless gesture. "That's standard protocol. When there are no parents or guardians, a minor child is surrendered to the territory."

"I know." Dark, dim memories of a cold bed and bland food, of stern, overworked women taking care of too many children threatened to well up. Memories she'd thought she'd forgotten. She didn't want that future for Toby. There was something about him, a sweetness, that grabbed at her heart. "Maybe you know of a family around here looking for a little boy?"

"Times are hard. Many folks are having a hard time providing for the kids they have, but I'll ask the sheriff. He knows everyone in this town, so he might know of someone."

"At least there's a chance." The boy's round face and owlish eyes flashed into her mind, an image of him staring at the wall and refusing to talk, refusing to trust. She would pray hard for him, she decided as a familiar man caught her eyes. He made his way into the room, dressed in a shaggy fur coat.

"Tom!" She took a step without realizing she'd stood. She was halfway across the dining room without realizing she'd left the table. She spun around, laughing at herself. "Elijah, I'll see you later. Thanks for the bacon." She held up the strip clutched in her good hand.

"Anytime, Miss Eberlee." He went to tip his hat to her, only to find he wasn't wearing one. Embarrassment crept across his chiseled face in a pink sweep.

He was funny. Her heart thumped an extra beat, likely in anticipation of being with Tom. He'd come to take her to see her new home.

He stood framed by the doorway with his bulky coat unbuttoned, his blue flannel shirt and red suspenders showing. Tension bunched along his jaw. Fury darkened his face. He did not look glad to see her.

Tom didn't look glad at all.

Chapter Five

"**W**hat are you doin' with *him?*" Tom demanded, beefy hands curled into fists. "Are you usin' my dime to see if you can land yourself a bigger fish than me?"

"Why, Tom." She surged forward, shocked by the words coming out of his mouth. This wasn't the greeting she'd been expecting. No smile of welcome, no light in his eyes when he gazed upon her. Then she remembered he didn't know her. They were strangers. She was determined to show him the woman she was. "In time you will come to know that I would never treat you that way. I'm hurt that you think I could," she said gently.

"Oh." Tendons stood out in his neck. He shot a cold, aggressive look the marshal's way. "You were eating with him."

"Yes, I was. He invited me over so I didn't have to sit alone, and I'm grateful." Her face heated, aware of curious diners watching. When she glanced back, the turmoil within her calmed the moment her eyes met Elijah's blue eyes.

He looked concerned, but he didn't need to be. She smiled at him to tell him so. Really, everything was going to be all right, but she wasn't sure he believed her and she felt a little lost. She wanted Tom to be a good man; she needed him to be. "Tom, it's your proposal that changed my life, and I'm so glad. That's what matters here."

"Guess I got all heated up." He shrugged, self-conscious and a little sheepish. His hazel gaze caught hers bashfully. "Can't hardly blame me. A pretty lady like you could have her pick of men."

"Don't try and soften me with flattery." But a smile broke through. "It's true a lady likes compliments."

"I'll keep that in mind." He had a charming smile and a farmer's homespun way. "Do you want to see your new home?"

"Very much." She fetched her coat from the large coat tree by the door, where she'd hung it last night to thaw, ice-driven from the near-blizzard conditions. Now, exactly why did that remind her of Elijah and the way he'd stayed at her side, shielding her from the brunt of the storm? Perhaps any woman would find him hard to forget. As for the snug, fond feeling building in her chest, that was a friendly feeling. Nothing when compared to what she would have with Tom.

"What's wrong with yer arm?" Tom's gravelly voice grated harshly. He didn't help her with her coat as she slipped into it, careful of her splint.

"I fell and apparently broke it, but don't worry, the doctor said it should heal just fine," she finished quickly, buttoning up her coat. "By the end of January, it will be good as new."

"Doctor?" His jaw snapped tight, and his polite tone was strained. "I didn't agree to pay for no doctor."

"I don't expect you to." She struggled with her mittens. Tom confused her. Perhaps he still feared she might take advantage of him, and it was true enough there were women in the world who thought nothing of such a thing. He would soon learn she was not one of them. He didn't open the door for her, so she grasped the knob and pulled. Below-zero temperatures hit her like a punch. "I've made arrangements with Dr. Frost to work off what I owe him."

"By doin' what exactly?" Hazel eyes turned stone hard.

"By cleaning his office." Now she *was* displeased with him. "I'm not that kind of woman, Tom. I would think you could tell simply by looking at me."

"Sorry." He flushed red and bowed his head. He appeared to be humbled, except for the strain snapping along his tight jaw. "I just saw you makin' cozy with that man at your table, and I thought the worst. Shouldna done that."

"No, and thank you. How about we make a pact?" She realized the only horse and vehicle tied at the hitching post had to be Tom's, so she swept snow off the sled's wooden seat with her sleeve before she sat.

"Instead of thinking the worst, we'll think the best of each other. Agreed?"

"Agreed." Tom shook snow out of a fur robe and handed it to her.

"I'm so glad you are to be my husband, Tom." She laid her mittened hand over his gloved one, willing her heart to feel. The spark of affection she longed for did not take root. Perhaps that would take time. "I can't wait for my new life with you to start."

"Me, either." The corners of his mouth relaxed. He untied the horse, who flinched when he came near. The horse's gray flesh rippled and the animal sidestepped.

"Git back here, you old nag." Tom's voice held a note of what sounded like affection. "I rescued her from a merchant on the road to Billings not long ago. She was pulling a big heavy wagon all by herself, and it was stuck in a mud bog."

He paused to sweep snow off his side of the seat and climbed in. "The merchant was beating her something terrible. If you look, you can see the scars on her flanks. Well, the poor thing couldn't pull that vehicle out of the mud—it would have taken a team of oxen—" He yanked the end of the fur robe over to cover him and snapped the reins. "So I offered the merchant cash for her outright. Twice what she was worth."

"That was kind of you, Tom." See, what a good man he was, saving an abused animal, she thought. She eased back against the seat, releasing a breath she didn't realize she'd been holding.

"It took her months to recover from her wounds."

He guided the horse down the street into the low morning sun. Shop fronts whipped by and windows glinted in the sunshine. "She took a lot of care and time, poor thing, but she survived."

"And now she has a good home. You did good, Tom."

"Oh, pshaw, it wasn't much." He blushed bashfully.

Rather cute, she decided, letting out another held-in breath. He had many good features. A high, intelligent forehead, a straight nose and a boyish smile that gave him a friendly quality, like a man she could feel comfortable with. "What is her name?"

"Maggie. I rescued her just in time, too, because my team died not long after. First one, then the other." His hands gripped the reins firmly with a capable air. "Old age. I couldn't stand to sell them when they became too infirm to do the work around the farm. My brother lent me one of his horses until Maggie was strong enough to do the hauling."

"That must have been a hard loss for you."

"It was. You get attached to the critters." Tom shrugged shyly.

"Yes, that's the way it is with horses." Snowy townscapes gave way to the crisp, clean shine of mantled prairie rolling ahead of them endlessly. "When Ma and I had to sell our mares, it was like losing part of the family."

"I know what you mean." His gaze caught hers and held, and in them she thought she saw the same hopes for a compatible and happy marriage. Perhaps he was lonely, the way she'd been. Perhaps he felt empty the way she did, wanting to spend her life loving someone.

They shared a smile, and she wished her heart would spark. She wanted to love him. She wanted it more than anything.

"That's our place up ahead." Tom's voice broke the spell as he nodded to the left. A small smudge darkened the white spread of prairie. As Maggie drew them nearer with the clip-clop of her steeled shoes on snow, the farm became clearer. First a rise of gray smoke, then the faded red side of a barn and finally the mare pulled them onto a rutted driveway.

For the first look at her new home, Christina scooted forward on the seat, straining to see around the curve of the lane. The barn came into view first, paint peeling, the structure listing to one side. Mud stained the lower boards and trailed to the other shed-like structures behind it. Covered pigpens, she realized, mostly by the smell.

"My brother lives over the rise of that hill." Tom gestured beyond the pigpens. "See the smoke? His wife is lookin' forward to havin' another lady around." Tom yanked on the reins, drawing Maggie to a sudden stop. "Here we are."

The garbage in the front yard caught her gaze. A rusted washtub full of fallen snow, used tin cans poked up through the mud, edges jagged. What looked like a burning pit, full of refuse waiting to be burned come spring, sat far too close to the sagging board steps leading to the door. No porch, just an unpainted, weathered shanty with a crooked stovepipe jutting out of a half-sloping roof. Obviously Tom had built only half the shanty, which was often the custom of a new homesteader, intending to add the second half of the home later when times were more prosperous.

Obviously that time had never arrived.

"It ain't much, but it's home." Tom rose from the seat and held out his hand to help her. "It's your home, now."

"I'm glad to be here." She scooted across the seat and planted her feet gingerly in the deep snow. "I talked to the minister." Tom left the horse standing in the bitter wind and hiked across a random board poking up through the snow. "Reverend Hadly can do the ceremony as quick as this afternoon."

"That soon?" She hated the wobble in her voice.

"Of course, I understand if that's a mite too quick." Tom veered to the right, away from the neglected-looking shanty. "I know you ladies like to have things right. Your dress all pressed and your hair done up. But if you're thinking you want to invite folks, say that marshal, then I have to put my foot down. It would hurt my feelin's to have you see him more. I'm sorry about it, but you can understand, right?"

"I—" She blinked, realizing he was taking her to see the barn first. "I had no plans to invite anyone to our wedding."

"Good. That's settled, at least." He slopped through ankle-deep mud and muscled open the barn door. "Maybe tomorrow afternoon would be better. We could say our vows and be home in time for you to feed the pigs."

"The pigs?" She heard them oinking and rustling in the shadows. *She* was supposed to feed them?

"I made it clear in my advertisement." Tom's voice hardened, or maybe it was just the darkness that made it seem so. Straw crackled beneath his boots as he lit a lantern. "I said I was a farmer. I was looking for a helpmate."

"I thought that meant keeping house, cooking, tending the garden." She searched through her mind but the words printed in the magazine hadn't led her to believe she would be doing heavy barn work.

"Yes, I want you to do all those things *and* the pigs." Tom blew out the match and tucked it into the drawer at the base of the lantern. "I was very clear. You aren't trying to renegotiate with me, are you?"

"No, but I—" Her hopes hit the ground. She didn't know what to say. Golden light pooled onto the dirty floor and onto the nearest crudely built pen where too many pigs were crammed in a too-small space. Blunt snouts poked out between the wooden rails to sniff in her direction. Several animals squealed in a high, threatening way at her.

"As you can see, it's too much work for one man. Since my brother took over his wife's parents' place, I've been hurtin'." Tom's beefy frame ambled closer and his voice gentled. "You coming here is an answer to my prayers."

"You are an answer to mine, too." *This isn't as bad*

as it seems and there's goodness in everyone, she reminded herself. Maybe Tom was overwhelmed with work, as he said. Maybe he needed a helpmate as much as she needed one and they could clean up this place and all would be well. It was a desperate thought, but it was all she had to cling to. "Maybe we can improve our lives together."

"I like the sound of that." Tom smiled and brushed snow from her hair, and the gesture made her pick up her hopes and pray this could work. "Now come along and I'll show you the shanty."

Elijah couldn't get the image of Christina and her fiancé out of his head. Tom Rutger clearly looked smitten with her as he'd driven away in his home-built sled. Who wouldn't be? All it took was one look, one smile and men fell like trees at her feet.

At least, that's what had happened to him. Elijah squinted against the late-morning sun and clomped up onto the boardwalk. He had to stop thinking about her. He had to stop his heart from caring. What he felt wasn't right. He just needed to exert a little more willpower and these feelings would fade. This was a little crush, that's all. Nothing serious.

"Good morning, Marshal." Arthur Lawson looked up from sweeping a light layer of snow off the walk in front of his mercantile. "Can you believe the storm last night?"

"It must be slowing down business. Not many folks are out and about yet."

"True, and it's one of my busiest days of the year." Arthur sent the last of the snow off the edge of the boardwalk, his work done. "Funny thing happened this morning. I opened my front door and found my boardwalk shoveled clean, like it had been done in the wee hours, with just this fine layer of snow drifted on the walk. Isn't that something? Someone did a kind deed. Now, what can I do for you? Have you finished your Christmas shopping?"

"In a way." He had no family to buy for. Other than the Christmas Eve church service, it was a holiday he spent alone. "Mind if I ask you a few questions?"

"Not at all. Come on in out of the cold." The man opened the door and leaned his shovel against the wall. "Would you like some coffee?"

"No, thanks." Elijah yanked off his gloves and held his hands out to the potbellied stove, puffing heat into the roomy store filled with tidy shelves and product displays. "Did you happen to see yesterday's accident?"

"No, I was busy with customers, but I heard all about it." Arthur shoved a lock of salt-and-pepper hair out of his eyes and poured a cup of coffee from the pot on the stove. "Caused quite a ruckus, and near to suppertime, too. I've never seen the street backed up like that. Heard a boy was injured. Any news on him?"

"The doc said he'll be okay. Before the accident, Les from the lumberyard saw the boy running out of this store like a bullet. Did you notice him in your store?"

"Well, I noticed a boy. Guess I didn't realize it was

the same one." Arthur took a sip of the steaming brew. "Little guy, say around eight or so, scrawny, ragged looking. Eyes were big as saucers when he was looking at all the foodstuffs."

"That would be the right kid." Hard to forget how fast Toby had put away an entire plate of food.

"I saw him take a handful of jerky from the container, right there, next to the pickle barrel." Arthur shook his head. "Oh, I saw him steal, all right. But a kid like that, one who looks as if he hasn't had a meal in a goodly while, I look the other way. Figure the Lord is good to me and has blessed my business. I can spare a few pieces of beef jerky."

This was why Elijah loved his job. He spent time dealing with the worst of humanity, but he'd had the privilege of seeing there was so much more to the human heart. "You're a good man, Arthur."

"No, I'm a father." The man set down his cup.

Would Elijah ever be a father one day, he wondered. Christina popped into his mind, her exquisite beauty, her kindness, the way she'd brought him to life. He had to stop tormenting himself with what was out of his reach. Even if she wasn't promised to another man, he didn't have to be a genius to know Christina Eberlee would never be his. "If Toby comes back to the store, will you get word to me?"

"Is he in some kind of trouble?"

"That's what I want to find out." Elijah pulled on his gloves. "A boy like that is too young to be on his own."

"He needs family. He needs love," Arthur agreed. "I'll keep a sharp eye out."

The shopkeeper's promise heartened him as he pushed out the door and into the frigid wind. Signs of Christmas surrounded him, but the shop displays he walked by didn't put him in the holiday spirit. Garlands and holly, Christmas trees and nativity scenes stared back at him through glass windows but didn't touch him. His heart had closed up, and he knew why.

He spotted a small gray mustang pulling a sled at the far end of the town, coming in from the east. Sunshine glanced off the drifts which hadn't been beaten down yet by traffic. Christina was probably in that sled, he guessed.

"Marshal." Doc Frost swept open his office door, a mug of steaming coffee in hand. "Come in out of the cold and have a cup with me."

"Can't say no to that. I scoured the town again this morning. No sign of Toby."

"Likely he curled up in someone's stable to ride out the storm. For all we know, he's still there, warm and safe. But I worry about that lump on his head. He needs to be watched." Sam ambled over to the row of clean cups on a shelf.

Elijah shut the door behind him and took off his hat, savoring the warmth from the stove. A small fir stood in the front corner of the room, undecorated, stuck in a makeshift tin can stand.

"My daughters insisted I bring it in this morning." Sam held out a mug, steam curling from the dark brew.

"We've had our tree up in the parlor for a week, but this one's stayed in the barn. Keep meaning to bring it in, but something always distracts me."

"Like medical emergencies?"

"Yes, those tend to crop up." Sam had the easygoing, relaxed humor of a man with everything—a loving wife, two darling twin girls and a happy home. It was nice to see. "Better have my nurse decorate that tree. Christmas will be here before you know it."

"It's a few days away." Elijah took a sip of coffee—black, strong and bracing. His gaze strayed over the cup's rim to the window, drawn by an inexplicable force. He saw Christina slide off the seat of Tom Rutger's sled and step onto the boardwalk. Her gaze caught his through the window.

"I'll come by for you tomorrow morning?" Tom Rutger's words rumbled faintly through the window. He hadn't offered her a hand down. "I'll speak with the minister."

"No… I mean, I'd rather have a Christmas Eve wedding," she said to Tom as she tore her gaze away from the window. Elijah tried not to hear her faint words muffled by the window and walls, but his ears strained for the sound. "Remember, I wrote in the letter? I wanted a few days to acclimate and to get to know you first."

"I don't remember that." Tom's jaw grated, his flat tone loud enough to hear plainly inside the doctor's office. His gaze shot through the window like a bullet.

Elijah took one step back. This really wasn't his

business. The conversation outside lowered to an indiscernible murmur. His pride took a hit when he spotted sympathy for him on the doc's face. The man must have guessed that he had feelings for Christina. And if Elijah had been that obvious, then anyone else might be able to guess, too. Even Christina.

"I'd like to see her go to a better man," Sam said, polishing off the dregs in his cup, looking thoughtful. "She's a real fine lady. Tenderhearted. You could tell that by the kindness she showed Toby."

"Well, you heard her." Elijah grabbed his hat and plopped it onto his head. "I know Christina, and she's given Tom her word. She's marrying him."

"She could always change her mind," Sam pointed out hopefully.

He was not going to let that hope in. Elijah set down his cup, barricading his heart. "Thanks for the coffee. I've got to find Toby. Won't feel right until I do."

"I worry about him, too," Sam said, nodding his approval.

Elijah wished he could avoid Christina as he charged out the door but she spun toward him. His spirit acknowledged her even as he forced his feet to carry him away. Her gaze burned like a brand on his back. "You accepted my proposal." Tom's terse words traveled on the inclement wind. "I have it in writing. You said you'd marry me, and you will."

"On Christmas Eve day." Her gentle answer held a firm note. Easy to imagine her with her chin up, standing her ground, but Elijah resisted the urge to look. He couldn't step in to help; likely that would only make matters worse for Christina. "You ain't changin' your mind about me, are ya?" Tom's tone turned plaintive and wounded. The sound of a man manipulating carried on the wind.

Elijah's stomach turned, trying not to listen. He wanted more for Christina, so much more. But she'd given her word, he knew, and she'd likely made a binding promise in her mail-order agreement, a financial agreement that could not be ignored. He paused at the intersection. It'd be smart to check the nearby alleys one more time. Since it was nearly noon, likely Toby would need to start searching for his next meal. Elijah couldn't help Christina with her marital situation, but he could help the homeless boy. He could make a difference for Toby.

Chapter Six

Lord, I don't know what to do. Christina sat quietly as the doctor finished putting the new and improved splint on her arm. Her visit with Tom hadn't gone as well as she'd hoped. There had been no sign of the man she'd been dreaming of. Tom hadn't bothered to gaze deeply into her eyes, he hadn't gentled his voice when he spoke to her and he never once mentioned his hope for love between them, as his letter proposing marriage had suggested.

She was disappointed. It wasn't his neglected farm or the shanty with yellowed curtains and the mud on the floor. Dirt could be scrubbed away, curtains could be washed and garbage could be picked up. It was a man's heart that mattered. She wanted to find the good in the man she'd promised to marry. She should be excited about their upcoming wedding.

Why couldn't she be? She'd been dreaming of standing beside her betrothed in the church on Christmas Eve day. Right now she should be having fun planning ways to decorate Tom's shanty—to take down the limp, yellowing curtains and make fresh ones out of cheerful yellow calico. To clean every inch of the dust and dirt that had accumulated until the floor shone. To piece a patchwork quilt for the bed in the corner and braid cheerful rag rugs for the floors. She wanted more than anything to make a home and a life with Tom. But why didn't it feel right?

"You remember what I said." The doctor pinned the end of gauze, his work done. "Don't overuse this arm. Any swelling or numbness, you come straight to me. I want to see you in two weeks just to check all is well and before you ask, don't think about the bill."

"I was hoping I could start working off my debt." She hopped off the chair, wishing her arm didn't ache so. "There's a layer of dust on your bookcases I'm itching to get at."

"Don't I know it. I'm so busy these days, I can't get everything done." Doc Frost's smile was inordinately kind. "The dust will keep until your bone is mended."

"I'm not sure how much time I will have after I'm m-married." She could hardly say the word. What other sign did she need that she was not ready to become Tom Rutger's wife?

"If that's the case, then the bill will be your husband's responsibility." The doctor winked, unhooking her coat from the wall peg. "Not sure how good of a duster he is, but beggars can't be choosers."

"Sorry, but not even humor can distract me when I've made up my mind." She took the garment from him, the wool soft against her fingers. "I'll be back with a dust cloth the day after Christmas. Here's fair warning. Not you or a legion of doctors will be strong enough to stop me."

"Well, if that's the case then I'd better stand back when I spot you coming."

"Good decision." She stepped into the front waiting area, where she'd spotted Elijah standing not thirty minutes before.

Every kind thing he'd done for her came back in one sweet wave. She needed his friendship right now, and maybe that was the problem. Maybe she found Tom lacking because in the back of her mind, without meaning to, she compared him to Elijah.

What man could measure up to the handsome marshal? That wasn't fair to Tom, and it wasn't right. That wasn't the kind of woman she wanted to be.

She thanked the doctor a final time and said goodbye. The boardwalks teemed with shoppers and errand runners now that the skies were clear. The hustle and bustle filled the street with a feeling of anticipation, and the jingle of bells on passing sleighs served as another reminder of the holiday. Christmas was days away.

So was her wedding.

"Where do you think you're going?" A rich, deep voice spoke from behind her, layered with friendliness and something that sounded like concern.

"Elijah." He made the day brighter. He hiked toward her, a brown-paper package in one hand, his capable shoulders broad and with a confident ring to his gait. In a dark Stetson, black coat and denims, he looked like everything good in the world, everything a man ought to be.

Everything a friend should be, she corrected herself. Even if her spirit sighed a little when he was near, he could never be anything more. She had promises to keep and he was not part of them. "I was heading back to my room. How about you?"

"Still on the hunt for Toby." A dimple dug into his lean cheek. "I can't get that boy out of my mind."

"Neither can I. There was something completely sweet about him." She remembered the boy and how he'd talked of his ma. "I think he was loved by his family, and it has to be hard for him to be alone. I'm glad you're looking for him, Elijah."

"Well, I've got to take a break for a bit." He paused, then said, "Speaking of which, I have a proposition for you."

"Really? I'm not the kind of lady who normally speaks to men with propositions," she quipped.

"Sure, but this here is an entirely appropriate proposition for an engaged woman." He held up a package he carried. "Here I have two sandwiches. One for me, and one as payment for a favor. I'm looking at two houses for sale, and I'm no expert on these things. I could use a woman's opinion."

"And you would pay me lunch for my opinion?" She so wasn't fooled. The strip of bacon she'd had for breakfast was long gone, and her stomach had been rumbling for the past hour. Tom hadn't offered her a meal, but perhaps he would feel more devoted to her once they were wed. She could only pray so. "I'm absolutely certain my opinion is not worth that much."

"Sorry to disagree with a lady, but you are wrong." The deep notes of Elijah's voice rumbled, tugging her one step closer.

She knew what he was doing, helping her the same way he'd helped Toby. Marshal Elijah Gable went around making a difference, helping where he could, committing random kindnesses and never expecting anything in return. It was the man he was.

"I am no good when it comes to comparing one house with another." Elijah leaned one muscled shoulder against a support pole, handsome enough to make any eligible female in the vicinity go dizzy. "I can run down an outlaw, outshoot and outride any criminal I've come across, but give me two kitchens to compare and I'm lost."

"I have every confidence in you." She'd like nothing more than to spend time with him, and she suspected her feelings just might go a little deeper than she thought. Really, how could she not care for him? Maybe without ever meaning to, and that was her problem. It was hard to see Tom's merits when Elijah's outshone him. She had to do the right thing. "I'd like to help you, really I would, but I have to consider Tom's feelings. We're marrying in two days."

"Sure, I know that." Elijah winced. "That doesn't change the fact that I could use help house hunting."

Oh, she knew exactly what he was up to, trying to feed her when her own fiancé hadn't given it a passing thought, but a girl had her pride. "You'll have to find someone else to give you her opinion on kitchens. You know I'm grateful for your friendship. You've done so much for me, but I have to think about what Tom would want."

"Right, you're not a single lady anymore. You need to think of your betrothed. I understand. It's not appropriate, you spending too much time with a bachelor." He took a step back. "I'm disappointed. Sure you don't want a sandwich anyway?"

"No, I'm sure you can find someone to share your lunch with. Maybe a pretty lady you're sweet on?"

"Me? No." At least she hadn't guessed, Elijah thought to himself. He'd hidden his feelings for her better than he'd thought. "Guess I'll see you around, Miss Eberlee."

"Good day to you, Marshal." Admiration and apology telegraphed across her porcelain face, a mix of emotions that he felt, too.

He walked away feeling like something was missing, that he'd fallen short. There would be no more spending time with her; he'd known it was coming. If only that knowledge could stop the ever-growing affection ruling his heart.

Love was all about timing. It was two people having the right feelings, felt in the right way at the correct moment in time. Even if there'd been no Tom Rutger and no engagement, Elijah feared he'd never be the man for Christina. What would a young lady like her, as beautiful inside and out, want with a lawman like him?

Tom was one blessed man. Elijah prayed the farmer knew it and after the wedding would treat Christina with the love and care she deserved.

"Elijah, did you get one of the houses?" Clint Kramer stopped his horse on the snowy street.

"Sure did." His new house had been nothing but empty echoes, and he wasn't sure how much a bachelor would fill it up. His fear was that his home would always feel empty, missing what mattered most. He leaned against the boardwalk's railing. The feed store behind him wasn't busy—only a few farmers were about, getting their feed purchased and errands done before the holidays. "I'm an official home owner and you and me are officially neighbors."

"So you decided on the house down the street from me? Good." Clint nodded his approval. "Wise choice. Are you moving in today?"

"Got furniture shopping to do."

"Say, I've been keeping an eye out for that boy." Clint leaned forward in his saddle. "I thought I had him, spotted him on the crowded boardwalk about a block from here, but it turned out to be a kid ducking school. I just came back from the schoolhouse."

"Thanks for looking."

"Don't spend all your days off working, buddy. My office can do the looking instead." Clint gathered his reins. "Well, my shift is nearly done. Want to meet at Bitsy's diner for supper tonight? Five o'clock sharp."

"Sounds good." Much better than eating at the boardinghouse where Christina was sure to be.

"We've got to celebrate you being a homeowner, and just in time for Christmas." Clint nudged his horse forward and tipped his hat. "See you later, Elijah."

"See ya." He came to the end of the boardwalk, stepped into the snow and spotted small footprints close to the side of the feed store. Fresh prints.

Could be any kid, he thought, except that school was still in progress on this last school day before Christmas break. He knelt to take a closer look at the print. About the right size, he decided, going down on one knee. Treads had worn off the shoe, just like Toby's had been, and that looked like the imprint from a string holding one shoe together.

Gotcha, he thought. His pulse beat a little faster as he followed the tracks round to the back of the store.

"Hey! What are ya doin' in my sled, boy!" A man's harsh shout echoed in the back lot. A man—was that Tom Rutger?—tossed down a fifty-pound sack of feed from his shoulder. "Put that down. Don't you steal from me."

Elijah bolted into a full-out run even before he saw a mop of dark blond hair bob up from the back of a homemade sled. Panic rounded the boy's green eyes. Brown paper crinkled and groceries went flying as the kid launched out of the sled. Quick as a flash, Tom reached beneath the sled's seat and a horsewhip snaked through the air, hissing and snapping.

"Ah!" Toby cried out with surprise. A stolen tin of crackers tumbled from his hand into the snow. The whip drew back, to lash again.

"Rutger!" Elijah shouted. "Don't you dare."

The whip sagged and Tom swore profusely in anger at missing the boy. Elijah darted around the sad-eyed mare, with more than a dozen healed whip marks on her flank. Something would have to be done about that later. All Elijah could see was Toby hightailing it down the alley. "Wait, Toby. It's me. Elijah."

"What's going on out here?" Devon Winters, the store owner, poked his head out the back door.

"Fetch the sheriff," Elijah ordered over his shoulder.

Toby ducked into the residential street, fast footing it between houses. Elijah gained ground and caught the boy by the collar behind a ramshackle stable. "Toby, why are you running from me?"

"I didn't w-want to get arrested." His little face scrunched up in defeat. "I'm a crook."

"Yes, I'm aware of that." Elijah propped his hands on his knees to catch his breath. "You nearly wore me out. I've caught criminals a lot slower than you."

"I am a criminal." Big emerald eyes rounded with fear. The cold wind stirred his unkempt sandy hair, tousling it around a lump, bruised and purple, near his temple. "I don't like it much."

"What do you think your ma and pa would think of you stealing?" Elijah kept his tone gentle.

"They'd be mighty disappointed even if I only took things cuz I was hungry." Toby's head hung. "That's why I do two good things for every bad one. I help real old ladies by carrying their heavy shopping bags. I shovel boardwalks. I know it don't make it right, but I don't got any money. No one will hire me cuz I'm a kid."

"I see." He thought of Arthur Lawson's mysteriously shoveled boardwalk in front of the mercantile. He couldn't say why that touched him, but it did. There was only one solution. "I'm afraid you're going to have to come with me."

"Are you gonna put me in chains?"

"No, as long as you promise not to run. I can't let a hardened criminal like you roam the streets of this law-abiding town." Elijah placed a hand on Toby's shoulder. A hard ridge of bone seemed to poke through his clothes.

Across the way, voices rose on the wind, the feed store owner arguing with Tom Rutger, who'd gone red in the face. Apparently the man had quite a temper. Elijah tried not to think what a life married to Tom might be for Christina while he steered Toby by the shoulder away from the scene.

"Did he get you with his whip?" Elijah asked as they crunched through the icy snow.

"Nope. I was too quick for 'im."

"I'm glad you didn't get hurt." Elijah wasn't sure if he could have stayed calm otherwise. He thought of the boy he'd been at Toby's age, growing up safe and loved with his family. That was before tragedy struck, before they were homeless, before they lost Ma. Every child's life should be safe and secure and happy. "Where did you learn to run like that?"

"At the orphanage. I could outrun everyone. I used to go round and round the yard next to the fence just practicing until I was so fast no one could catch me."

"Who would be chasing you?"

"There was this one big boy. He was a bully. He'd pound on you if he caught you. Sometimes it was the lady in charge. If something bad happened, like a dish got broke or you spilled your bucket of water on wash day, she'd take the cane to the first kid she could catch."

"I see." The way Toby blew out a troubled sigh made him believe the boy. Toby may be many things, but he didn't seem to be a liar. "So you don't have any family anywhere? Not even a cousin or a grandmother?"

"Don't know. The orphanage couldn't find none." Toby stopped, stock-still in the lane. "What's jail like?"

"Well, there are bars on the doors and windows." Elijah nudged him down an alley. "The good part about jail is you get three meals a day."

"Good meals or bad ones?"

"Good ones."

"Marshal?" Toby's hand crept into Elijah's. "Am I goin' to your jail?"

"For now. Nothing scary is going to happen to you, I promise." He guided the boy between buildings and they emerged onto the boardwalk next to the Range Rider territorial office. "We have to wait and see what the sheriff says. He has jurisdiction over the town. I'm a lawman for the territory. So you'll wait here with me to see what he wants to do. How does that sound?"

"Okay. I'm real sorry. I don't like stealin'."

"I know." He remembered being homeless and sleeping under the stars rolled up in blankets, hunger gnawing through him, making it impossible to sleep. He opened the door. "Go sit by the stove and warm up. We'll see if I can't talk Burke, the other marshal, into running up to the bakery for us. How does that sound?"

"Real fine, sir." Toby looked so little as he ambled across the office and sat by the red-hot stove.

Elijah had no idea what he was going to do with the boy. Send him back to an orphanage? No, that didn't sound like the best option. Unless he could think of something else, it was the only one he had.

Christina missed Elijah, wishing she could have gone with him to look at houses. She didn't mean to wonder how he was, but he filled her thoughts even when she tried to stop them. Just like she couldn't help picturing what spending the afternoon with him would have been like. They would have laughed, they would have talked, they would have shared smiles and little jokes.

That's the connection she wanted with Tom. Every time she thought of him, her heart felt like a boulder, sliding farther and farther down in her chest. She had to believe once she knew him better and saw more of his heart, her doubts would vanish.

There was only one problem. She didn't love Tom. How did you make your heart fall for someone? Could you think your way into love? Or was her lack of feeling a sign that their marriage wouldn't be a happy one?

No, not that. Her step faltered and she grabbed a railing for support. *Please let him be the man I need,* she thought. *Please let him be a good husband.* A flake of snow danced in on the wind and brushed her cheek. Was it a reassurance from heaven? Or a warning? She'd been so certain that Tom would be exactly the man she'd read about in his advertisement.

Across the street, she spotted a familiar gray mare. Tom was still in town? She crossed the street, wanting to see him, needing to see if she could will her heart to feel. She spotted him through the window in the sheriff's office. Was something wrong? She skidded to a stop on the boardwalk, watching through the perfect frame of glass as Tom launched out of a chair, fury like a rash on his face. He stormed toward the door in a temper, threw the door open so hard it crashed against the wall and rattled windowpanes.

She stared at the raging man, big and frightening. "Filthy little beggar," Tom yelled over his shoulder. "And I'm the one you bring in? What kind of rotten sheriff—" He spotted her, he skidded to a stop and clenched his rough hands into angry fists. "What are you doin' here?"

"Walking back from the church," she said, staring at him. He vibrated with rage and yet before her eyes he willed it from him like a chameleon. The strain washed from his face. His eyes went from rampant to placid.

"But it's not Sunday." He plunged his hands into his coat pockets, perhaps to disguise they were still clenched into fists. "What were you doin' at church?"

"I wanted to meet the minister, since he will be marrying us." She felt uneasy with Tom. All that rage, where had it come from? Where had it gone? "What are you doing in the sheriff's office?"

"I was nearly robbed today and that blasted—"

"Tom!" she exclaimed. He'd sworn, something he'd written in his letter he never did.

"Pardon me for swearing." Anger leaked out in a huff, and as if remembering himself he blew out a breath, rearranged his face and tried again. "I meant to say, I was carrying a sack of pig feed out to my sled and found someone going through my groceries. Worthless riffraff, just helping himself to what's mine."

"Worthless riffraff?" That was no way to talk about another human being. "If someone was stealing groceries, perhaps they were in need—"

"Not my concern." He untied the mare, who took a step away from him. "I was innocent, but the sheriff hauled me in like a criminal. They just let that kid—"

"What kid?" Christina asked, but she knew anyway. A bad feeling gripped her stomach.

"Oh, some filthy kid."

"Did he have green eyes, sandy hair and a black coat?" She knew it was true even when Tom didn't answer. She couldn't believe it. The way he'd spoken of Toby, a little boy, made her blink back tears. "You didn't press charges against him, did you? Is he safe with the sheriff?"

"You're worried about that kid and not me?" Tom yanked hard on the reins. Too hard. The mare whinnied in pain. "You're my intended, Christina. You accepted my proposal. I deserve your respect. You need to be worried about my feelings, not some—"

"You didn't answer my question, Tom." Disappointment hit her hard. She staggered, clutching the hitching post for support. He wasn't a good man. He wasn't the husband she needed. "I saw you talking with the sheriff, but I didn't see Toby. Where is he? Answer me."

"Let's get this straight right here and now." He rose up greater than his nearly six-foot height. "You don't give the orders around here. Now get in the sled. I'll drive you to Mildred's."

"I'd rather walk." The wind shifted, driving icy flakes into her face. They caught on her lashes and struck her cheeks like tears. Tom was not her knight in shining armor. He was not the man he'd promised to be.

"You disappoint me. You're not the woman I expected." Tom marched around the far side of the mare, lost in the swirl of newly falling snow.

What was happening to her life? It was supposed to be getting better, but instead it felt as if it were falling apart. She watched Tom hop into the sled, snap the reins and the gray mare lunged forward, pulling him away from the boardwalk until the haze of the storm swallowed him.

"He wasn't being honest with you, miss." A deep voice boomed with sympathy. The sheriff stood in the open doorway, the door Tom had left open when he'd stomped from the office. "That wasn't what happened with Toby."

"Is he all right?"

"Sure, he is. He's a few doors down with the marshal. Just so you know, Tom tried to use a whip on the boy. Toby says he wasn't hurt, but if he had been, I'd have thrown Tom in jail." The sheriff's tone left no doubt about that. "There's something else. Not many folks know this, but I'm the sheriff around here so I make it my business to keep an eye on things. You are the third lady come to town to marry Tom. Last summer, a woman was here three days and got back on the train. A second lady fled after a week."

"Oh." She hadn't expected Tom's lies about the other women he'd proposed to. Tom had called himself a good, Christian gentleman in his advertisement. She'd expected more of a man who called himself a Christian.

"You need anything, miss, you come by anytime." The lawman gripped the knob, ready to shut the door. "My office will help any way we can."

For some reason, the sheriff's kindness hurt like a blow. He was offering her a hand because they both knew she couldn't marry Tom Rutger. There would be no Christmas Eve wedding, no happy marriage, no one to love and no home of her own. Her dreams shattered as quietly as the snow falling in the street. She was alone again.

Chapter Seven

"Christina?" Elijah's heart stopped at the sight of her standing in the swirling cold, gripping the boardwalk rail as if the thin piece of wood was all that kept her upright. He left Toby by the warmth of the stove and fled into the cold with no coat or hat to stave off the blast of northern wind.

"Are you all right?" he called out.

Of course she wasn't. Dumb thing to say. He rolled his eyes. He'd been so preoccupied with Toby's situation that he hadn't been watching out the front window. If he had, he might have noticed what had stolen her smile.

She didn't answer. She didn't look up. As he marched closer, his boot strikes muffled by the fast-accumulating layer of white, she squared her slim shoulders and forced the sadness from her eyes. Pure, true blue gazed back at him and he felt a spark in his soul.

"Marshal Gable." Her forehead creased in adorable

furrows, just visible beneath her cap. "I hear Toby had a scare. I'm so sorry for my fiancé's role in it."

"The kid will be all right. Something tells me he's endured worse. He's wolfing down an early supper." Keeping a respectful distance, he gestured toward the office window, two doors down. "We're trying to sort out the problem of what to do with him for the night. I haven't contacted the territorial agency yet."

"You're sending him to an orphanage?" She breezed closer.

"That's protocol. Not much I can do about it," he answered, doing his best to sound distant instead of concerned. It was tough trying not to care so much for her; it was tearing his heart out. "For tonight, we're waiting. All it takes is a telegraph from Helena, and he's on the train to the closest orphanage."

"I've been praying for a home for him." Sadness layered her voice. "Maybe it's not meant to be."

"I hate to think so." Elijah held the door open for her when a wind gust rattled it. "I volunteered to find him a place for the night. No one in our office has room for him. The sheriff has offered his sofa, but I was hoping Toby could stay with someone he knew. I was going to check if Mildred had an unrented room she could spare."

"She's booked full. I overheard her saying so this morning when I came up for breakfast."

"Well, so much for that."

"I could take him." She tugged off her cap, static crackling through the soft cloud of her hair. Rich brown satin that shone almost russet in the late-day's light. "My room is small, but we could make up a bed on the floor."

"It's a kind offer." Relief filled him. He strode into the office, hardly feeling the winter's chill because Christina was at his side. "Toby, look who's here."

The kid looked up, spotted Christina and blushed berry red. A piece of boiled potato dropped off his fork and he bowed his head, hiding his expression. "Howdy, Miss Christina."

"It's good to see you again, my friend." She settled beside him on the bench. "The last time our paths crossed, you ran away before I could make good on a promise."

"Oh." His face turned a deeper shade of crimson. "Sorry."

"I've been worried about you." She peeled off one worn mitten and the other. "I've even been praying for you."

"You have?" The boy slumped as if in defeat. "I wish you hadn'ta done that."

"Why not?" Christina asked in her gentle way.

Toby shrugged, misery curving his narrow shoulders. He stared at his plate, unable or unwilling to speak.

"Well, I'm going to make good on my chocolate cake promise," she declared in the tone of a woman not used to being thwarted. "No one is going to stop me this time."

No answer. The boy stared at the food on his plate, but made no move to eat it.

"Toby, if I were you, I'd give in. Christina is a woman on a mission," Elijah said, pouring a cup of tea for the lady.

"Yes, never stand in the way of me and a mission," Christina agreed. Humor curved in the corners of her mouth, chasing away the sadness he'd seen earlier, but he knew it was there. He knew something was wrong.

He wished he had the right to help her. He wished she wanted him to be there for her, but her earlier words to him had been clear. He had to respect that. "I can help with your chocolate cake mission."

"Excellent." She took the cup he offered. "We'll get Toby settled in my room at the boardinghouse."

"What?" The kid's head shot up. Wide eyes filled with panic.

"It'll be okay." Elijah used his most reassuring voice. "Nothing bad will happen to you. You'll be safe with Christina, and I'll be right upstairs. Plus, there are those two pieces of chocolate cake to think about."

Toby bit his lip, looking like his world had ended. Funny, dessert usually had a different effect on kids.

Elijah ruffled the boy's hair, and a fatherly sort of tenderness touched him. Surprised him more than anything could. "Go ahead, and finish up your meal. Then we'll head over to the boardinghouse."

"I was gonna sweep up here first," Toby said around a mouthful of meat loaf. "I'm a real good sweeper."

"I'm sure you are. But we've got Burke for that," Elijah said.

"Hey, I heard that," came an answer from the far corner, where the other marshal sat, finishing up his daily paperwork.

"So finish up eating, kid, but I need your most solemn promises. One that you can't break."

"Whadda I hafta promise?" Toby swallowed hard, his fork landing on his plate with a clink.

"You can't run away like last time. Do you understand?" Elijah thought of all the dangers in the world to a boy alone. "I mean to help you, and so does Christina. Can you stay and trust us to do that?"

He felt the blaze of her gaze on him and the weight of her quiet scrutiny. He did his best to hide his tenderness from her.

"Okay, I promise. It's gotta be better than the lean-to at the feed store." Toby hopped off the bench and landed with a two-footed thump. He set down his empty plate, the lamplight emphasizing a spattering of freckles across his nose. "I'll be real good, Miss Christina."

"I know you will." She set aside her teacup to smooth the tangle of hair from his forehead. The kind gesture moved Elijah in a way he couldn't explain.

"Does you arm hurt real bad?" Toby's eyes shone with the sadness of an old man's, as if he carried the weight of the world.

"Not anymore. The swelling has gone down and I

can move my fingers, see?" She demonstrated with a dazzling smile.

"I'm real sorry you got hurt."

"That's sweet of you, but I'll be as good as new in no time, don't you worry."

Toby was a good kid. He just needed a chance. Elijah shrugged into his coat, surprised at the idea taking root. He couldn't help thinking of his house and all those empty rooms. He wanted to talk over the pros and cons with Christina but he couldn't reach out to her. She needed distance between them, and that's what he'd give her. He opened the door, careful not to look at her.

"Thanks, Elijah." Toby gazed up at him, buttoning his coat. "It ain't better being alone."

"No, it's not." He rubbed the top of the kid's head, not sure at all what he was feeling, but he feared a decision had been made without his being really aware of it.

"Oh, Elijah." Christina stopped in the threshold, a knowing look in her eyes, as if she could see his thoughts. She looked at him, as if he'd hung the moon and the sun. "I can't believe what you are going to do."

His chest cinched tight in one painful twist. The love he'd been holding back? It crashed free like a dam breaking, drowning him in a flash flood.

Rotten timing, he thought. That's what the two of them had. He watched her join Toby on the boardwalk, the wind dancing through her hair, the cold wind kissing her face. It felt like dying to try to reel in his affections, but he failed. No, nothing, not even his iron will could drive the warmth from his heart. It was here to stay. She would marry another, he would spot her in town or in church with her husband, and later with their children.

From a distance and through the years to come, he knew he would always love her.

"And I get to sleep in here?" Toby grasped the door frame, as if afraid to step into Christina's room. He took in the coal heater, the comfortable armchairs and the numerous quilts folded on the trunk beneath the small window. "It's like a dream like this."

"Every once in a while dreams come true." Christina knelt beside the narrow straw tick Elijah had brought out of storage, thanks to Mildred, and tucked the top sheet into a tidy corner fold. "You never know what good turn your life is about to take."

"If you hope for that all the time, then you just get disappointed." Toby leaned against the doorjamb, still not able to make eye contact with her. "Good things don't last long."

"Sometimes that's true, but not always." She shook out a quilt and spread it across the sheet. "But when I was a little girl in the orphanage, I was so unhappy and afraid."

"You were an orphan, too?"

"And then I was adopted when I was three, almost four. My new parents were wonderful, but they could only afford one child." She smoothed the wrinkles from the quilt, feeling the old hurt behind her eyes. She'd desperately missed her sisters, who'd been left behind. She could hardly remember their faces, and the loss of the locket with the images of them hurt like a spear to the chest. It felt as if her past was truly gone, as if the last link to her family was broken.

And with what she knew about Tom and his wish for a barn worker as a wife, she feared there might not be a happy family in her future.

"I seen kids adopted where I was." Toby took one hesitant step in, as if afraid to believe, afraid to trust. "Some of the men and ladies looked like they'd be real nice to a boy, but none of 'em ever picked me."

"I can't think why not." She tucked the end of the quilt beneath the mattress and stood. "You seem like a fantastic little boy to me."

"I ain't little anymore." Toby's chin shot up, like a tough man of the world. "I can take care of myself."

"You don't have to worry about that for tonight." She plumped a pillow and set it in place. "There. That should be comfortable for you. Can you tell me what happened today with the man and the whip?"

"He caught me digging in his groceries. He was real scary, but I was in the wrong." Toby reluctantly plunked down on the chair.

"It was an actual horsewhip?" Her insides went cold at the thought, remembering the scars on the gray mare's flanks and Tom's heroic story of rescuing the horse.

"Yep. He pulled it out from beneath the seat." Toby's face heated. "I jump real fast so he missed me."

"A grown man should never take a whip to a child." Molten-hot anger bubbled in her stomach. The sheriff's words returned to her, reminding her she wasn't the only woman duped by Tom's seeming honesty. "I'm glad you weren't hurt."

"Me, too." The lump near Toby's temple was almost gone, the bruise yellowing.

"What do you want to be when you grow up?" she asked.

"A blacksmith. I like banging things with a hammer, and I like horses real well. I can look in their eyes and know what they're feelin', so I think I'd be real good at smithin'. If someone would show me how, I could do it. Then I wouldn't hafta go back to the orphanage."

"The territory isn't going to let a child live on his own." Elijah strode into the room and into the spill of light. "Someone has to look out for you, Toby."

"You mean, like the lady at the orphanage?" He bit his bottom lip. *What a sweetie,* Christina thought, with those honest clear eyes and freckles. With his tousled, flyaway hair and boyish vulnerability.

"Maybe we can find someone better than that lady. That's what I promised to try to do, right?" Elijah handed over a dinner plate with two generous slices of chocolate cake. "Fresh from the dining room. Mildred cut them big especially for you."

"Oh, thank you." Toby's eyes went as wide as saucers. He grabbed up the fork and dug it into the nearest chunk of cake. "Would you really find someone better?"

"You have my word of honor." Elijah's reassurance rang low and trustworthy, a promise made to always be kept, to always be held true. "You can count on me, Toby. Right?"

"Okay." Toby swallowed hard. Trusting didn't come easy to him, but he was trying.

She turned her back, trying not to let her admiration for the man build any higher or it just might knock the roof off the boardinghouse. One day a woman was going to capture his interest, and she would be everything he deserved—lovely, kind and devoted. As beautiful as he was handsome, and suited to his upstanding position in the community. Christina's chest tightened, thinking of that future. She wanted the best for him. She didn't know why her heart ached so.

"I'll go fetch more coal." Elijah left the boy to his dessert. He couldn't meet her gaze either as he slipped by her, seemingly taking up all the space in the narrow room. "I'm sure you two are settled for the night and then I'll get out of your way."

"And I'll do my best to keep him from going out the window." She followed him into the hall, into the alcove at the base of the staircase. Sounds from the lobby and dining room filled the air. "Maybe you should know. You're not in the way."

"Okay." He hesitated with one foot on the bottom step. "Thank you for taking him."

"It's no problem."

"I'll be right back."

"Okay." Her gaze caught his, for one brief moment, and he thought he saw the flicker of something in her eyes, but before he could be sure it was gone. He hoped for another glimpse of it as he climbed the stairs, keeping her in his sight for as long as he could. She looked oddly sad, but there was not one sign that she felt anything more for him. They were allies helping Toby. That was all it could ever be between them. Now, they were not even friends.

"Marshal." Mildred swept away from the tree standing in the corner of the lobby, freshly cut and scenting the air. "There you are. Will you be staying with us for Christmas? So many of our residents are leaving to be with family. I'm trying to get an estimate for the kitchen staff."

"I haven't gotten around to telling you, since I'm paid until the end of the month." He studied the tree, green boughs uplifted, waiting to be decorated. Looked like he'd have to get one of those, too. It wouldn't be a proper Christmas in his house without one. "I bought a house. I'm moving in tomorrow."

"How wonderful for you!" Mildred beamed her approval. "I'm so happy for you, Elijah."

"Thanks. I plan to live in Angel Falls for a long time." Life was all about timing. Everything happened in God's time, and he felt that the Lord was leading him to a purpose, to a life that would no longer be lived alone.

When he opened the back door to grab a pail of

coal from the lean-to, the faint melody of voices echoed through the alley. The storm snatched most of the words, but he recognized a Christmas carol and stopped to listen to a few bars before heading back inside.

"You go grab dear Christina and that sweet little boy and I'll take care of the coal," Mildred ordered as soon as he stepped foot into the lobby. "Go on, quick. Bless Reverend Hadly and his choir. They know how to spread Christmas cheer."

"Is that music I hear?" Christina asked, appearing on the landing, buttoning her coat. Toby followed in her wake, wiping chocolate crumbs from his face on his ragged sleeve. "I love carolers. For years I belonged to our church choir and on snowy evenings before Christmas we would sing our way through town."

"Hurry!" Mildred called, heading for the front door. "You don't want to miss this!"

"Then we better not." Elijah wanted to take Christina by the hand and lead her to the door, the wish as natural as breathing. "Let's go listen together."

"I'd like that." She smiled up at him, making his heart stop. He didn't know how he made it to the door, which he held open for her and the boy. He followed them into the brunt of the winter storm and stood at Christina's side. She seemed enraptured by the half circle of two-dozen singers, men and women, in four-part harmony.

"Come all ye faithful," the voices rang out. "Joyful and triumphant."

"Oh, they're lovely." She didn't seem to realize she was the lovely one, giving Toby her mittens because he had none to warm his hands. She stood beside him like a mother, a hand on his shoulder, perhaps so he couldn't dart away. "Do you know this song, Toby?"

"Uh-huh." The boy nodded.

"Come and behold Him," Christina sang in a soprano nearly as sweet as she was. "Born the king of angels."

"Oh, come let us adore Him," Elijah joined in. "Oh, come let us adore Him—"

"Christ the Lord," Christina chimed, so dear, it wasn't his fault that his hands slipped around her cold fingers and warmed them. It was the only thing he could do for her, such a small thing when his devotion to her was great.

One perfect moment, Elijah thought, standing beside her, for this one moment they were together.

Chapter Eight

"Toby?" Christina looked up from her morning work sweeping dust and evergreen needles into the dustpan. "What are you doing?"

"I'm helpin'." The boy took charge of her broom and gave it a sweep. Dust flew upward, scattering across the hallway. Head down, Toby swept in fast, practiced strokes.

"Hey, that's my job." She left the dustpan where it lay to rescue the broom. "You are supposed to be getting ready to go with Elijah."

"I am ready." Face scrubbed, teeth brushed, hair combed, he looked less like the runaway and more a little schoolboy. "Can the marshal really find a good home for me?"

"He said he could. I know Elijah." It felt as if she'd always known him. "He's a man of his word."

"I want to be like him when I get big." He held on tight, refusing to let her wrench the broom from his grip. "He's tall and he's good."

"He's very good." She ignored the twist of emotion, the one threatening to keep her heart from beating. Images from last night flashed into her mind, of Elijah towering beside her in the dark, of his mellow baritone rumbling in song, of his hands warming hers.

It was gratitude and a lot of respect, she felt, that was all. Surely it was nothing more.

"There, I done it." Toby grinned, proud of himself, at the end of the dim hallway. "And I gotta whole lotta dirt, too."

"Guess you need the dustpan." She scooped it up, careful not to let the dust inside whirl away. "Thanks for helping, although Mildred hired me to do it."

"You got a job here?"

"For now." She knelt to set the dustpan on the floor. "I'm filling in for the downstairs maid until she gets back from her Christmas trip."

"Did she go to see her ma and pa?" Toby asked.

"Probably." She took the broom from him and brushed the debris into the pan with a few efficient sweeps. "I hear footsteps on the stairs. It's probably Elijah come with good news."

"I dunno, Miss Christina. I'm not gonna hope until I see good things for sure."

It wasn't the marshal who stepped into the spill of morning light. Tom Rutger took one look at the child and scowled. "What's that runt doin' here?"

"Toby, would you please go in my room and shut the door?" She left the dustpan and stood. "Promise me you'll wait for me there."

"Yes, ma'am." A wary look pinched his face as he darted around Tom. The door closed with a click.

"What are you doing with him?" Tom's tone darkened. "You know what he did to me."

"He's a child with nowhere to go. I had hoped you would have compassion for him." She opened the small closet door beneath the staircase and put the broom away. "In fact, I had hoped you would be a lot of things. I'm glad you came by, because we need to talk."

"I didn't come to talk. We need to get some things straight." Muscles strained along his jaw. "I chose you cuz you needed a place to live. Figured you'd be the grateful sort to have a man to provide for you."

"I am grateful." Dreams of her new life had sustained her on the nights hidden away in an alley or a stall trying to sleep. Daydreams of the happiness she would make with Tom, the man who'd offered her a new life, had brightened her days on the journey west. Tom had given her hope. "I had dreamed you would be the man I needed, but you're not, Tom. I could never marry a man who takes a whip to a little boy."

"But he was stealin' from me." Fury drew him up like a bear.

"I know, but that doesn't make trying to whip him right." She wished things could be different for them. If only Tom had been honest with her—and himself. "If you were the man I'd prayed for, then you would know why it wasn't right."

"A lot of things ain't right. You aren't at all the nice lady I thought you'd be. We need to straighten that out." Cords strained in his neck. "A wife ought to show the proper respect to her husband. You need to apologize to me, and that will help make things right."

"I can't, Tom. I can't marry you." She could see him for who he was. She'd seen beneath the self-deprecating mask he wore to the troubled man beneath. She felt sorry he was so lost. "You have no notion how much I had wanted this to work."

"What are you talking about?" His forehead furrowed. "You need a roof over your head and I need help with the farm. We made a fair deal."

"It would be, but I can't marry you. I'm so sorry." Kindly, she laid her hand on his forearm. "I don't think we're compatible. Do you?"

"No. You're strong-minded. You didn't say a thing about that in your letter." He shook off her touch. "I've learned to handle strong-minded creatures, and I need help with the pigs. That's why I need you. You'll marry me, or return what I spent on you."

The costs of her room and the train ticket. She nodded. "Of course, I will. I'll pay you as soon as—"

"Not good enough." He dug into his coat pocket and hauled out her letter. "Remember I asked you to put it in writing? You agreed to marry me or pay on demand what I loaned you for the trip here. It ought to be binding, as I learned from the last lady who came here on my dime and decided I wasn't good enough for her."

"But I don't have the money right now."

"You have until tomorrow at noon or we wed. It's as simple as that."

She watched him storm up the steps and disappear from sight. Tom's ultimatum rang in her head. He wouldn't let her out of their marriage bargain. He'd never intended to try to love her. There had never been the chance to belong to someone and to be loved. All Tom had ever intended to give her was shelter and meals. Was that her future? Bleakness hit with the bone-breaking force of a blacksmith's hammer.

"Christina?" The door creaked open and Toby stared at her through the crack, his eyes filled with tears. "Do you really have to marry that man?"

"I don't know. I think so." She leaned against the wall since her knees had gone weak. "The train ticket and my hotel add up to a lot of money. It would take a long time for me to earn it all."

"I'm real sorry." He pulled the door open wide enough to slip through, not making a sound. He clutched his coat in his hand. "It's my fault, cuz I—"

"You are not to blame." No way did she want him to think so, even for an instant. "A grown man should never take a whip to a child. End of story. I'm sorry he frightened you, but look at it this way. I owe you greatly because now I know the man Tom truly is."

Toby gripped his coat pocket firmly, as if holding on to something inside. Misery and guilt were written across his freckled face. "That's not it, I—"

Footsteps knelled on the stairs. A man's voice called down the stairwell, "Toby, are you ready to go to your new home?"

"Elijah." She didn't want to accept the wash of

peace that flowed through her when he strode into sight. It wouldn't be right to acknowledge the feelings that had been building for so long, feelings which were really more than respect and admiration, a great deal more than friendship. "How did your morning go?"

"Better than expected." A full smile carved across his granite features. Snow clung to dark strands of his thick hair, as if he were touched by grace, and standing in his black coat and denims, he was her dream.

Just once, she wanted to know what it would be like to experience a dream, a real one, one that would never fade or change or show a different side. She felt her smile light her up. "Better than expected? Does that mean—"

"That's right. Heard back from my friend at the governor's office. They intend to arrange an inspection of the orphanage Toby came from, but for now, I have the solution I'd hoped for."

"Just in time for Christmas." If she couldn't have her Christmas wish come true, then she gave thanks to the Lord that her wish for Toby had. "Would you mind if I tagged along?"

"It wouldn't be the same without you." Kindheartedness radiated from him. He flashed his amazing smile at her. "After all, we found him in the street together."

"And it feels right to see him to the end together." She matched Elijah's smile. She wasn't going to think about her future, that lurking darkness. She ducked past him, ignoring the sweet pull of his presence on her soul. "Let me grab my coat."

"We'll wait." The warmth in Elijah's tone faded. Only then did she realize Toby hadn't said a word. He stood in the hallway staring at the string holding his shoe together.

Elijah's gaze snared hers. He'd noticed it, too. He held her coat for her, aiding her with the sleeve. His knuckles grazed the back of her neck and she shivered from his nearness. A harmless crush, she told herself, that was all. She couldn't wish for more.

"What's wrong, Toby?" Elijah moved away from her and knelt down, eye level with the boy. "Are you afraid I'm going to trick you and take you back to the orphanage?"

Toby shook his head once, his sandy hair tumbling forward to hide his eyes.

"Are you afraid your new pa won't like you?"

"Sorta, but that's not it." Toby sighed, downcast.

"Are you worried you won't like the new home I found for you? Tell me what's troubling you. I'll do my best to help."

"I don't deserve a new home." Toby choked down a sob. "Not at all."

"Of course, you do. The plans are already made. I got the temporary approval from Helena. You have to come with me." The kid would be all right once he saw where he was going. He buttoned the boy's coat. "Let's go."

"I'm very curious to see the place Elijah found for

you." Christina tugged on her knit cap, bundled up for the storm. "I have a feeling it's going to be great."

"Now let's not get his expectations up too high." Elijah found himself laughing, taking the boy by the hand. "I'd hate for him to be disappointed."

"Impossible." Her certainty touched him deeply. She swept up the stairs, leading the way into the light. The Christmas tree blazed in the lobby and the glass angel on top seemed to watch over them with her hands clasped and golden gowns flowing as they pushed through the doors and into the storm.

Nothing felt more right than walking with Christina at his side. The snow fell too hard to speak, so they walked in silence. He kept Toby's hand firmly in his and blocked the brunt of the wind from Christina. He made sure she didn't hit a patch of ice when she hopped off the boardwalk and into the street. He pretended for one brief second that she could be rightly his.

Love filled his heart with the sweetest longing. Love lit his soul with the strongest devotion. If he could have any wish come true this Christmas, it would be to make Christina his. To slip a ring on her finger, to make her his wife and offer her everything he had. His home, his heart, his life. He would never be whole without her.

Timing, he reminded himself, as he pulled the keys from his pocket and unlocked the front door to his new house. Timing was everything. He held his heart in check as he opened the door.

"I love your house," Christina said. Her footsteps

echoed in the empty parlor, her skirts rustled as she spun around taking in the details—gray stone fireplace, big windows with window seats and polished wood floors that gleamed. "I can just picture it. Furniture, curtains, a fire blazing in the hearth. It will be a wonderful place for you and Toby."

"I'm gonna live *here?*" The boy's jaw dropped. "You're gonna be my pa?"

"If that's all right with you." Elijah went down on one knee to better gauge the kid's reaction. "What do you think?"

"I think you'd make a mighty good pa." Tears stood in green eyes. "But maybe you don't want a boy like me."

"Maybe I do." There were those fatherly feelings again, filling him up. Looked like his life was about to change. Now he had a family when his life had been empty for so long. "Do you know the first thing we're going to do? Head over to Lawson's and get you everything you need. New shoes, new clothes." Toby swiped his tears away with a frayed sleeve.

"And a tree, too," Elijah added, climbing to his feet. "We'll need presents to go under it. What do you say, Christina? We could use a woman's help with our shopping. We're men. We don't know where to start."

"That's what the shopkeeper is for." She knew what he was asking her, and she couldn't do it. It would hurt too much. Seeing Elijah accept Toby broke the last of her control over her heart.

This was a daydream, a moment out of time. She'd been a fool to think she could have more. "I promised

Mildred I would help her this afternoon. She's short-handed, since two of her maids are on holiday, so no shopping trip for me. Toby, I'm thankful you have a home."

"Me, too. I can't believe it." The child didn't meet her gaze. His face flamed red again. "Maybe I'm just dreamin'."

"Not a chance." She smoothed flyaway strands of his hair. "You'll see. Some good things last. It's okay to believe."

Toby swallowed hard, nodding once. She turned away, too tangled up with emotion to say more. This was goodbye. Their paths—hers, Toby's and Elijah's—would take different turns.

From this point on maybe she'd spot them in church and smile, or see them on the boardwalk and wave. But her life was no longer hers. She owed Tom a debt she couldn't pay. The only honorable way out was to marry him. "Goodbye, Elijah."

"It's been a pleasure knowing you." Something great and luminous flickered in his blue gaze. Something that looked like love.

"No, the pleasure has been all mine." It took all her will to force her feet to take her from him. Every step she took felt like a blow, one wound on top of another. Icy snow needled her face as she tripped down the front steps and into the storm. For all the years to come, she would never forget Elijah's kindness or his goodness. She would always keep a piece of their time together alive and safe in her heart.

Chapter Nine

"How do those feel?" Arthur Lawson asked, kneeling in front of a silent Toby.

The boy nodded once, refusing to make eye contact with the shopkeeper.

"They look pretty good." Arthur pressed his thumb against the leather, feeling for Toby's big toe. "Got some growing room in there, but not too much. Why don't you take a walk around the store and test them out."

Toby nodded, his gaze downcast, and trudged off, circling around the pickle barrel. Elijah watched, his heart strangely full. More shoppers scurried in, shaking off the effects of the storm. Near white-out conditions blanketed the view of the street, but it gave the world a Christmassy feel.

Christmas. While he appreciated the reason for the season and celebrated Christmas Eve at the church's candlelight service, he always spent the day alone.

But not this Christmas.

"Arthur, I need gifts and things for a stocking." He wanted to get this holiday right, including a tree to decorate. "I haven't had a reason to do much celebrating Christmas Day, not since my pa passed, almost a decade now."

"Then you're talking to the right man. I can help. I noticed how your boy looks at the train set in the window every time he walks by. Watch."

Sure enough, as Toby made a loop around the store his gaze strayed to the window where a train sat on wooden tracks in front of a shiny red depot. Town buildings and peg people and wooden horses lined the track. A boy could spend many hours in play with that gift. Elijah nodded. "Then it's a sale."

"I'll throw in some Christmas candy for a stocking." Arthur kept his voice low as Toby returned. The man knelt to check the shoes, and Elijah's mind wandered.

What about Christina? She'd looked as if she belonged in his house, looking at home in the parlor, and the image stuck with him. The distant toot of the afternoon train arriving sounded faintly, reminding him of the time. The afternoon was speeding by and his new furniture would be delivered in a bit. When he dragged his attention to Toby, the boy stood red-faced, shaking his head at whatever Arthur was saying to him.

"I think these will serve you well, young man." Arthur gathered the neatly folded stack of clothes they'd picked for the kid. "If you need anything else, you be sure and let me know. I'll do my best to help you, son."

"You're real nice," Toby muttered, staring at his

new shoes. "I feel real bad. There's somethin' I gotta tell you."

"Oh, what's that?"

"I was real hungry when I first got off the train." Toby gulped, gathering his courage. "I stole three pieces of beef jerky from the jar over there."

"Is that so?"

"I'm awful sorry. Please don't get mad." Toby braced himself as if expecting a blow. "I swept up your boardwalk so you wouldn't have to."

"Ah, so you're the mysterious snow clearer." Arthur moved behind the counter to tear off a length of brown paper from the roll. He sent Elijah a wink. "Here's how it's going to go. From now on, we start fresh. You pay for anything you take out of this store, and we stay friends. Agreed?"

Toby blew out a breath of relief. "And I'll shovel off your boardwalk for as long as you want so I can make up for stealing from you."

"How about until school starts up again?" Elijah gave the kid's shoulder a squeeze of approval. "That seems long enough to make up for what you did. What do you say, Arthur?"

"Sounds good to me." Arthur smiled as he tied a string around the paper, securing it with a bow.

"You did a good job, Toby, fessing up." Elijah watched as the kid's head bobbed downward again. He still looked miserable as he shuffled up to take one of the two packages Arthur handed him. Something else was bothering the boy.

Elijah took the heavier package, paid for the Christmas gifts Arthur promised to deliver after closing and steered Toby through the doors. The jingle of harness bells rang dully through the thick snowfall. Only faint shadows through the white hinted at the horses and sleighs passing on the street. Determined shoppers were out, clogging up the boardwalk and radiating tension. So much to do, with tomorrow being Christmas Eve.

"You and I need to get back to the house." Elijah turned, but Toby wasn't there. He was a few paces back, slumped against the mercantile wall. Tears spiked the boy's lashes.

Maybe this was overwhelming for him. Maybe he was missing the parents he'd lost. Elijah backtracked. "Hey, there. You don't look all right."

"Nope." Toby choked out. "If I told you what I done, you won't want me to live with you no more."

"Well, now, you'll just have to tell me and see." He leaned against the siding, too. "I'm in an understanding mood, so you just go ahead and say it."

"I didn't mean to h-hurt her." Toby's head bobbed forward until his chin touched his chest. "I wouldn't want to hurt no one, not ever."

"I believe that." Elijah knelt down so he was eye level. This was his first real test as a pa, and he didn't want to fail. "Who got hurt?"

"Miss Christina." His voice sounded small, wobbling with misery.

"So, you were the boy I couldn't catch that day at

the train stop." It had been snowing and the kid had such a head start that Elijah hadn't seen more than a faded red hat and a dark coat disappearing around the train engine. Now it all made sense—why the boy had run, why he blushed around Christina. "You knocked into her pretty hard. Was it your first reticule snatching?"

He nodded vigorously. "I bumped harder than I figured—I didn't mean it. I didn't know she was hurt until I seen her in the doctor's office."

"And that's why you ran away. That's why you were afraid I was going to arrest you."

"But she didn't know it was me, so I felt badder and badder. She kept being nice to me." Toby blinked hard, refusing to let his tears fall. "Are you gonna put me in jail now?"

"You need to make things right, but you already know that." Elijah wished his thoughts didn't veer off to her. Was she preparing for her wedding? Maybe pressing her dress, figuring out how to wear her hair? It tore his heart out, leaving him in utter darkness.

He couldn't let her marry another, not without letting her know how he felt.

Do I have a chance, Lord? He stared at the heavy snow, obscuring all view of the sky. Heaven felt so very far away.

"I wish I could do more for you, but I run the place—I don't own it anymore." Mildred circled behind the front desk. "If you can't pay cash for the night, then I can't offer you credit."

"I understand. I had to ask." Christina wasn't surprised, but she'd hoped. Already the sun had gone down. Night had fallen, and it was still storming.

"Personally, I don't see the harm in letting you stay one night, since the room would stay empty anyhow. What's a night between friends, but my boss doesn't see things that way. There's rules I have to follow."

"Rules are rules. I understand." Christina set the door key on the scarred countertop. Tom had refused to pay for the night's lodging after she'd tried canceling their wedding.

"But our bargain still stands. You'll be cleaning for me tomorrow morning?"

"Absolutely. You have no idea how grateful I am."

"It was nothing." Mildred tucked the room key away reluctantly. "I'll see you tomorrow and be sure and come in early for breakfast. You've earned it. Do you have a place to stay tonight?"

"Don't you worry about me. I'll get by." She'd swung by the livery stable on her way through town earlier and checked out the stalls and the entrances. For the six months she'd been homeless, she'd learned a thing or two about finding shelter. "You have a good evening, Mildred."

The storm battered her when she crossed the street. The quick supper she had sat like a stone in her middle as she wove down an empty street, then a vacant

alley and pried the wooden latch on the livery's back
door with her button hook.

The moment she eased through the door, the rela-
tive warmth of the stable surrounded her. Horses in
their stalls craned their necks, coming up to their gates
to take a look at the newcomer. She reassured them
softly; they nickered in return and went back to their
business of eating grain or drowsing contentedly.

It didn't take long to locate a few clean horse blankets. She was grateful to the livery owner for the thick
bed of fresh straw in an empty corner stall. Her injured
arm ached from the cold, but soon she was tucked beneath the wool blankets and getting warmer. As the
wind gusted against the siding like an eerie song, Elijah filled her thoughts.

Was he tucked safely in his house? Had his furniture been delivered? Did he and Toby sit down at their
new table to say grace over a hot meal? How were they
passing the evening? Reading? Getting Toby settled
in his new room? Sitting before the hearth sharing
stories?

She prayed for it to be so. If her soul longed again
for the sight of Elijah's smile, she had to ignore it. She
had to let him go. Her feelings ran deep for him, deeper
than she could allow herself to acknowledge. It would
be wrong to give in to her affections. She owed Tom
a debt, one she could only repay by marrying him.
Her only way out would be to talk him into letting
her work off what she owed him in his barn instead

of marrying her. She wasn't sure he was the type of man to consider a compromise.

A creak of the front door opening rocketed through the silence. She sat up, pulse pounding. Was it the stable owner? Or the local law? Dreading the image of Sheriff Kramer, or worse, Elijah, she bolted to her feet, the straw rustling tellingly. What did she do? Did she hide and hope to remain undetected? Or did she run?

Footsteps padded across the hard-packed floor. She held her breath, heart banging against her ribs. No, it was too late to run for it; she'd be spotted. With no other choice, she silently grabbed her satchel and crept carefully into darkest corner of the stall. Maybe the shadows would hide her. She waited, trying not to imagine the worst—being discovered, being trussed up and marched to jail, being locked behind steel bars for trespassing. She did *not* want to explain to Elijah why she'd been arrested.

A match flared to life at the front of the livery. The clink of a glass lantern chimney echoed, and the horses stirred, drowning out all other sounds. She waited, fighting against the rise in her soul, the way it rose whenever the marshal was near. Was it Elijah, or her wishful thinking?

Memories of him filled her mind. How he'd made her laugh on the train, how he'd watched over her, how she'd never felt more safe with anyone. The midnight-blue gaze, the curve of his chiseled mouth and the lilt of her heart when he'd taken her hand. The affection she'd tried to fight, the caring she had denied, fought for light. She had to wrestle it back into the dark. She feared what she felt for Elijah could never be.

"Hey, Miss Christina, are you here?" A boy's familiar whisper cut into her ruminations.

"Toby." She gripped the side of the stall, standing on shaky legs. "Why aren't you home with the marshal?"

"Cuz I promised him I'd make all the things I'd done right." He spotted her and rushed over. "That's why I'm here."

"How did you know where to find me?"

"When the boardinghouse lady said you'd left, I knew where you'd gone. There's no place warmer than a stable with animals in it, when you've got no place to go." Toby opened the stall gate, so little, so sad. "It's all my fault. I broke your arm."

"No, you didn't. How could you say such a thing? I fell, and it didn't even happen here in town." Then her gaze fell on something he pulled out of his old coat pocket—a faded red knit cap. She could barely see it in the ambient light from the distant lantern. She recognized that hat. Not that she'd gotten a look at the boy who'd slammed into her on the train platform that day, but he'd been about Toby's height. He'd worn a dark coat. "It was you. You stole my reticule."

"Yep, I did and I wished I hadn't." He bowed his head in shame. "I never meant to hurt you. I wished I hadn't done it as soon as I did."

"I see." She took a breath, letting the realization sink in. It should feel like betrayal. She should be furious or hurt. But those feelings weren't the ones building within her. "You must have been desperate to do such a thing and pretty disappointed to discover there wasn't even a penny inside."

"Nope, you were broke." Toby sniffled. "I tossed your reticule out when the train was moving, so I can't give it back."

"Oh." He hadn't kept it. The treasures within were gone, the remembrances of her loved ones.

"Can you f-forgive me?" The light found him, illuminating the earnest need for absolution. Honest green eyes pleaded. "I wouldn't blame ya if you couldn't."

"Of course I can." She knelt in the straw and held out her arms. Toby rushed into them, and she hugged him, savoring his little boy sweetness. She ached for a happy family of her own, a wish that felt out of reach.

Wasn't that life? Some dreams you lost, some dreams you reached. Only God was in charge.

She let Toby go. "You don't have to steal anymore, Toby. The marshal is going to take care of you."

"That's what he told me and I believe him." Toby rubbed at his eyes. "I don't know what I done to get so lucky. But I prayed real hard for a long time, before I gave up. Just the way my ma taught me."

"Then it's not luck that Elijah came into your life." She brushed a lock of hair out of his eyes.

"Not luck at all." Boots thudded close and light spilled far down the aisle, the lantern held in a man's strong hand. The shadow behind it took on shape. First she saw a hint of wide shoulders and the crown of a Stetson. Everything around her vanished in comparison.

Elijah strode forcefully into the aisle—carved granite face, high cheekbones, iron jaw. "Guess Toby was right. He knew how to find you."

"I—" The man stole her breath. He scrambled her thoughts. He made the wishes within her whisper, longing to come true. "Why are you here? I thought we'd said our goodbyes."

"Not even close." His dark blue gaze gentled, softening with affection. Affection for her? She could only stare, taking it all in, the breathtaking combination of steely man and loving heart. He leaned closer. "You and I are not finished yet."

"We aren't?" Hope took wing inside her. Why couldn't she breathe properly? His closeness stole every speck of air in the stable as she wished. How she wished.

"Miss Christina? I got somethin' for you. It was here a minute ago." Toby dug deep into his pocket. The bump of his hand followed the garment's lining; perhaps there was a hole in the pocket seam. The lantern light fell on what Toby pulled from his pocket. Gold glinted like a sign from above.

"My adoptive mother's brooch." She couldn't believe it. Happiness rolled through her at the sight of the treasures. "My sisters' locket. You kept them."

"I had to. After I got kicked by the horse and you

helped me, too, I kept 'em." Toby swallowed hard, holding the jewelry out to her. "I couldn't pawn 'em."

"This is the best Christmas gift I've ever received. Thank you." The beloved brooch felt familiar in her hands. She traced the gold filigree edging and the soft ivory cameo. With it came the legacy of her adoptive mother's love, the woman who'd raised her with care and gentleness. "You have no notion what this means to me."

The gold locket opened with a small click and she took out the image, her gaze drinking in the sight of her two sisters, their image lost no more. Realization washed over her. "I'm not sure how much I can get for this jewelry and it will be hard to pawn them, but, Toby, you may have just given me my freedom from Tom. Oh, you dear boy."

"No need to sell your treasures," Elijah answered, hanging the lantern on a post nail. "I stopped by Tom's place on my way here. That's why we tracked you down."

"You talked with Tom?" Her pulse skidded to a stop. "Why would you do that?"

"Because I care what happens to you." The light in his deep blue gaze made her hope. His granite features gentled. "I paid your debt to him."

"What? Oh, Elijah, no. It was so much money. I—" Words failed her. Why had he done that for her? Tears burned behind her eyes as her hopes began to build.

"You were worth it, Christina. Whether you marry Tom or not is now entirely up to you." Elijah towered over her, so close he scrambled her senses, drowning out all things but him. Only him. His warm hands gathered hers, engulfing them with his strength, with what felt like tenderness.

"It's a lot of money, Elijah," she choked out. "How can I let a debt stand between us?"

"Because it was no debt. I did it—" He paused. Emotion lit him up, where shadows had lingered before. "Well, I did it out of love. That kind of act can't be reimbursed. It's not a debt to be owed. You just have to accept it."

"Out of love?" She studied him—mountain-tough, rugged and strong. The kind of man who kept his promises, who stood for what was right, who had captured her unwilling heart with his every kindness. From the very first moment she'd met him, she'd prayed for a husband like him, for a man with his true heart to love her forever. That prayer wasn't about to be answered, was it?

"I love you, Christina." Abiding affection warmed the low notes of his voice. Honesty shone in his adoring gaze. "From the moment I first set eyes on you, you changed my heart. You brought me back to life. You made me see what my future could be. I don't know how you feel about me, but I have to ask. Do you think you can come to love me, too?"

His words were a gift, as precious as a blessing from above. His question stymied her. He had no notion that he'd touched her heart the same way.

"No," she said gently. "I don't think there's a way I can come to love you. Because I already do."

"You do?" He winced, thankfulness carving into his face. He looked as if he couldn't believe it, as if he'd just received the best gift of all.

"I do. I love you, Elijah." The words felt freeing. Joyous.

"Then I have a question to ask you." He went down on one knee. "You traveled a long way to find a husband, and I'm hoping it's me. Will you do me the honor of being my wife? Will you marry me?"

"Marry you? I would love nothing more." She laid her hand against the slant of his jaw, tenderness lifting her up with a power she'd never known before. "Elijah Gable, you are the best Christmas gift I could ever have."

"Now that's where you're wrong." He rose, towering over her and wrapped her into his arms. "You are the best gift, the very best. I'll spend the rest of my life showing you just how much I love you. I promise you that."

It was a vow she believed. Enduring love filled her soul. His arms closed around her, holding her close. *Prayers do come true,* she thought, *and sometimes in the way you never imagined.*

Maybe those were the best-answered prayers of all. She snuggled against Elijah's strong chest, listening to the beat of his heart. She'd traveled to Montana Territory looking for a home, but she'd found more.

She'd found true love.

Epilogue

One year later, Christmas Eve

"Go lay down in your bed, Paddy," she told the bright-eyed dog and pointed toward the gray stone hearth. The banked fire radiated enough heat to keep the mutt warm through the night. Paddy turned and ambled toward his bed, nails clicking on the hardwood. He circled three times and eased onto his blanket. He closed his eyes with a sigh.

Christina spun in place, checking the parlor one more time, making sure everything was in place. The stockings were hung and filled. The tree in front of the window stood guard over the presents piled beneath its boughs. Tomorrow, it would be alive with candle-light watching over their festivities. A turkey would be roasting in the oven, pies would be set out to cool and later she would tap out Christmas carols on the piano in the corner.

"He went out like a light." Elijah lowered his voice,

his boots padding lightly on the stairs. "He was sound asleep the moment his head hit the pillow."

"It was a busy day for him." She was thankful that Toby was thriving. The boy excelled at school; he'd been a wonderful son and was now a happy boy. She still marveled how the three of them found one another, three strangers brought to Angel Falls on the same train. Love had made them a family. Deeply grateful, she turned toward her husband, toward the man she loved. Her heart filled with bliss when he opened his arms to draw her against his strong chest.

"It was a big day for all of us." His lips brushed the top of her head. "Last-minute shopping, caroling, candlelight service."

"Yes, today was the second-best Christmas Eve of my life." She leaned back in his arms, gazing up at his handsome face. At the granite cheekbones, midnight eyes and iron jaw. She could never get enough of him. He was her heart, her soul, her everything.

"It was my second-best Christmas Eve, too," he agreed. "Hard to top last year."

"When we were married." Bells had tolled joyfully when the ceremony was through. The moment they had emerged from the church, hand in hand and heart to heart, sunshine had broken through the storm to greet them like a blessing from above. The last year had been like a dream spent as Elijah's wife and as Toby's adoptive mother, the best days of her life.

More were still to come. She placed her hand on the rounded bowl of her stomach. Their baby would be here by June. In the meantime there were wee clothes to sew, booties and blankets to knit, and flawless days to share with the ones she loved. She caught sight of the beautiful doily her friend Annabelle had sent for a Christmas gift. She hoped Annabelle liked the table runner she'd crocheted just for her. Their friendship remained strong, two former mail-order brides who'd found the adventures of their lives traveling to Montana Territory.

"I hope you don't have any regrets in choosing me," Elijah asked.

"Only one." She pressed her cheek into his touch. Humor burnished her, made her radiant, made her luminous. "We have only this lifetime to spend together. It doesn't seem long enough."

"Then we'd better make every moment count." It was a promise he vowed to keep every day of their lives, with all his might, until his last breath. She was his life, his everything. There wasn't anything he wouldn't do for her. She made his life whole.

Brimming over with love for his treasured wife, he kissed her tenderly. Love was all about timing, he thought, and gave thanks that it was their time for happiness.

* * * * *

Dear Reader,

Welcome back to my second novella with fellow author and good friend Janet Tronstad. We had so much fun writing our previous *Mail-Order Christmas Brides*, how could we not band together for a sequel? So, band together we did. Once again our heroines meet on the train west and become great friends while riding the rails, wondering about their lives to come as mail-order brides. My heroine, Christina, is robbed at a train stop when she gets out to stretch her legs and who should come to her aid but handsome Marshal Elijah Gable? Elijah is everything she prays that her fiancé will be…a dream, a blessing and a forever home for her heart. It turns out Tom Rutger is nothing of the same, but her hand is already promised to him. How can her story end happily? I hope you enjoy this Christmas tale where love triumphs, everyone finds a home and God's grace shines so brightly.

Thank you for reading *Home for Christmas*.

Wishing you peace, joy and love this holiday season,

Jillian Hart

Questions for Discussion

1. What was your first impression of Elijah? How would you describe him? What do you like most about his character?

2. How would you describe Christina and Elijah's first meeting? What did you learn about her character? What did you learn about Elijah? What makes you care for him?

3. What do you feel for Toby? What motivates him to run away? What shows you the kind of boy he truly is?

4. When Tom and Christina first meet, how do you know Tom isn't the right man for her? What clues do you see? What others do you see as the story progresses? What sort of man do you think Tom really is?

5. What is the story's predominant imagery? How does it contribute to the meaning of the story? Of the romance?

6. Do you see God at work in this story? What meaning do you find there?

7. How would you describe Elijah's faith? How would you describe Christina's faith?

8. What do you think Elijah and Christina have each learned about love?

SNOWFLAKES
FOR DRY CREEK

Janet Tronstad

With love to my niece, Sara Enger.

Whoso findeth a wife findeth a good thing,
and obtaineth favor from the Lord.
　　　　　　　—Proverbs 18:22

Chapter One

Montana Territory, December 1885

Gray clouds hung low in the sky as a distant rumble
sounded in Gabe Stone's ears. Tiny bits of hail hit the
brim of his Stetson and bounced off to fall on the two
children standing beside him on the railroad platform
in Miles City, an old military town halfway between
Fort Keogh and Dry Creek in the Montana Territory.
The day was bitter cold, but that wasn't what bothered
Gabe. He looked at the passenger train rolling steadily
down the tracks toward them and frowned. Annabelle
Hester, his brother's mail-order bride, was coming on
that train and Gabe would have to say *something* to
her. He just didn't know what yet.

"I hope your pa had sense enough to send her a
round-trip ticket," Gabe muttered as he bent to lift the
collar on four-year-old Eliza's coat. Even as he said it,
he knew the return ticket wasn't likely to have been

purchased. His brother, Adam Stone, never believed his plans could fail—not even when he was the one causing them to do so.

Eliza didn't say anything, but her eyes grew big in a face still round with pink baby sweetness.

Daniel, her scowling seven-year-old brother, wasn't as shy as she was and he tugged on Gabe's jacket.

"Pa said she's going to be our new ma," the boy announced when he had Gabe's full attention. Daniel's chin jutted out, fierce determination on his small, thin face. "Annabelle doesn't need any more tickets. She's staying with us."

"That's Miss Hester to you," Gabe said, hoping to change the conversation. He paused to wipe the hail off Daniel's hair. He didn't quite know what to tell his niece and nephew any more than he knew what to say to the woman. "Where's that scarf that I gave you anyway?"

Daniel hung his head at that and Gabe's gaze moved over to Eliza. He should have known. Edges of the brown knit scarf were barely visible under the girl's frayed coat. The boy was clutching a ragged muslin quilt around his shoulders. He'd claimed, when Gabe had asked him earlier, that he was warm enough, but Gabe could see now that there were more holes than padding in that quilt.

He took off his wool jacket and draped it around the boy. The garment was so big it almost touched the platform, but it would keep out the damp and cold. He didn't want either of the children to get sick; they had enough trouble in their young lives at the moment.

Gabe looked back at the train and his frown deepened. When it came to trouble, they all had enough. His brother had ridden off this morning before dawn, leaving behind a note saying he'd made a mistake. Adam claimed he couldn't face a new bride-to-be when his heart was still full of grief over his late wife's death. Then he asked Gabe to take care of dealing with the woman on the train for him as though she was nothing more than a bit of unwanted lace that needed returning to some distant place back East.

They were all silent for a moment and then Gabe heard his nephew catch his breath. It sounded like the boy was struggling to hold back a sob.

"But she said we were to call her Annabelle." Daniel's voice wavered at the start, but then rose stronger as he lifted his teary gaze. His eyes flashed in defiance before he faltered again and whispered, "Until we feel easy with calling her Ma." He stopped in apparent embarrassment at his emotion and brushed at his eyes. "Pa said, too."

Daniel had gathered up the woman's letters this morning and insisted on bringing them to the station— almost as though the sight of her written words would stop her from turning around and leaving. He had already seen too many promises broken in life and he would take this one hard. Gabe wondered if the boy understood just how much he and his sister needed someone.

"Miss Hester might not be staying long," Gabe said as gently as he could, moving his hand down to rest on his nephew's hunched shoulder. The truth was best spoken aloud even if no one wanted to hear it. "But you have me to take care of you."

No smiles or squeals of delight greeted his promise to them. Both children stood looking at the raw planks of the platform. Their backs were to the train depot.

He didn't blame them for not being particularly pleased with his words. They were still grieving their mother's death from pneumonia this past spring and were likely bewildered at the changes in their father. They barely knew Gabe, even though he was their uncle, and it was unlikely their father had said anything nice about him. He had to do what he could for them, though.

Still, he shook his head. He thought his brother understood what could happen when he told him that some of the women in town were suggesting the two little ones would be better off if they were put up for adoption. Adam always had been stubborn. When he brought his children here several months ago in an open wagon, he refused to stay with Gabe, preferring to keep his grudge against his brother going even if it meant he had to make camp by the creek with his children. He pretended they were on some picnic and not just sitting there with no shelter as the nights got colder, but the townswomen knew better. They had even figured out how many nights Adam had left the children by themselves so he could go off drinking and gambling.

"It'll be all right," Gabe said, putting a hand on Eliza's soft hair.

Snow had come early this year and Gabe had finally shamed his brother into moving the children to the old trading post he had inherited from their father. He wished it could have been different. He understood everyone's grief all too well. When he was nine years old, his mother had sickened and died, too. His father had given up and sent Adam back East to be raised by their grandmother. Gabe, being judged old enough to work, was kept.

Gabe had begged his father to let his younger brother stay, saying he would work enough for both of them. But their father refused. Even though twenty-five years had passed since then, Adam still blamed Gabe for not stopping their father. Gabe wondered, too, if he had done enough.

Those bitter memories faded as the boy in front of him stepped closer to his sister.

"Pa promised that Annabelle was going to stay with us," Daniel repeated fiercely.

"For Christmas," Eliza added, her voice barely audible.

Today was December 21 and Gabe had heard his brother say those very words every day for the past week. There wouldn't be any presents, Adam had warned the children, but they would have a new mother to make up for it.

"Well, he ought not to have said that," Gabe told them flatly. His brother hadn't said much to him since he and the children moved into the trading post, but one night, when he had run out of neighbors willing to buy him a drink and had stumbled home earlier than usual, he had talked about his land up north. Adam said he had tried to keep things going there without his wife. But his one cow had died, the fields had proven too dry to plow and the roof on his sod house had collapsed. The marker on his wife's grave had even blown down.

"Annabelle sent her picture and everything," Eliza reminded Gabe as they stood there.

He nodded. Adam had been sober the day he'd shown him the woman's photograph and Gabe had hope for the first time that his brother might find the strength to start a new life. A grieving love that made a man unable to do what he had to do was something his brother couldn't afford. He had been proud when he showed off the image of his new bride.

Annabelle was a real lady in the picture, wearing one of those fancy feathered hats in a wild rose color with all the little ribbon curls and jeweled flowers women back East liked. The hat was big enough to hide most of her face and she was looking away from the camera. Only a wisp of brown hair was allowed to escape along a fine-boned jawline. She was the kind of woman Adam would make an effort to please, Gabe told himself. His brother would stop drinking for her.

Maybe she could even turn them all into a normal family.

Just then the train braked to a stop in front of the depot.

There were a dozen or so other men around. Gabe let them hurry forward and call out their greetings as the passengers started getting off the train. Finally he saw Miss Hester step down from the last railroad car.

"She's wearing her hat," Eliza said, her voice rising in excitement as she looked up at Gabe. He nodded. His heart was thumping inside him. The photograph hadn't prepared him. Why, she was beautiful—and delicate in a way that made him nervous. She might be the kind of woman to give Adam a new life, but Gabe was more comfortable with the sturdy women he knew in the West. They could take disappointment. Even from a distance, Annabelle looked like a tender flower. What if she fainted when he told her his brother was gone? Or cried? Gabe might not know much about children, but he knew less about ladies like her.

If the children hadn't dragged him forward, he would have just stood there, hoping his brother would suddenly appear and save them all from what promised to be a disaster. All Gabe could think about was that he hadn't taken time this morning to put a fresh handkerchief in his pocket. His mother, bless her memory, would have reminded him to get one if she'd been there as he got the children ready to leave the trading post. Adam always had a clean handkerchief. He'd be ready to meet anyone, even someone he was destined to disappoint.

The smoke of the train floated down on Annabelle and she brushed the dark specks off her shoulders before putting her hand up to her hat to be sure it was secure. She'd breathed soot for days and it was a relief to be outside even though the cold made her breath catch. She pulled her heavy knit shawl tight. This morning, she'd changed into her gray silk dress, the only good one she had that wasn't made of black mourning cloth. By now it was wrinkled, though, and her arm had started to ache from being pressed against the window.

For reassurance, she turned to look back at the friend she had made on the journey out here. Christina Eberlee looked out the window of the train and waved. Annabelle lifted her hand in response. Christina was a mail-order bride, too, and they had both shared their dreams, and worries, as the train sped down the tracks.

Annabelle turned around then, still feeling the swaying of the train. She wanted Christina to be happy for her and she knew her friend would like to glimpse her promised husband.

The flakes of snow were falling faster, but Annabelle could see well enough as she looked around. There were quite a few men on the platform and she searched eagerly for a lanky blond rancher who was handsome enough to make her blush just thinking about him. Adam had written a description of himself so she would be able to identify him. He hadn't said he was handsome, of course, but he had indicated he was well-received so she figured he was finely made. Besides, she'd let Christina read some of his letters and they both agreed that Adam had a flirtatious tone in his letters that men got when women had been telling them they were good-looking since the day they were born.

Annabelle tried not to squint as she continued looking. Most of the men wore hats of some kind, but she didn't see anyone who was likely to be her fiancé. Then she saw the children. Adam hadn't been able to send a picture of them, either, but he had described them to her.

Just looking at the two sweet darlings filled Annabelle's heart with hope. She had never expected to have a husband and children. Her father always said she was a drab bird, all brown like a little barn hen, and that men liked women who had strong colors like a strutting peacock. He ignored the fact that it was the male of that species that had the vivid feathers. Instead, he'd gone on to say that the best she had to offer a man was her usefulness. Learn how to cook good plain food, he'd advised, and don't shirk the heavy work in a household.

Ironically, over the years, her father had chased away what few suitors she'd had. He claimed the men were not interested in her but only in the store she'd inherit someday. He'd sooner part with her than his mercantile. As it turned out, he was right. When he died in the fire that both injured her and destroyed that store and their home above it, none of her old beaux came forward to ask how she was doing. A couple of them did send their condolences about the loss of the store, though.

Alone and homeless at thirty years of age, Annabelle didn't know what to do. All of her father's wealth had been inside the store so all that was left was a blackened square of land. A cousin said she could stay with him and his wife as long as she needed. They were almost as poor as she was, however, and, because of the way the burn scars on her arm had healed, she wouldn't be able to do enough to carry her share of the load. She refused to be a burden to anyone.

She didn't have to worry about that now, though, she told herself. She had a new life with a handsome, prosperous man who understood she couldn't do any heavy lifting and still valued her. She smiled to herself. The best was coming soon. Christina had assured her she'd feel a shiver of something fluttery around her heart when she met her future husband. That, the other woman had said with a giggle, was when she'd know she was looking at her true love.

Annabelle stepped toward the children, half expecting Adam to slip around the station building and surprise her. She knew that men wanted a certain dignity in their wives so she tried to keep her steps small and her curiosity hidden. A mail-order bride had no reason to expect true love, she knew, but on the journey here she had begun to hope for more than an arrangement of convenience.

When she reached the children, they were both beaming up at her.

"Daniel." She smiled at the boy first and then opened her arms to the girl.

The warmth of the children's greetings gratified her. She heard the sound of the train pulling away from the station and glanced up to wave at Christina again. At least her friend had been able to see the boy and girl.

Annabelle turned slightly to look some more, but she still didn't find Adam. The children were not alone, though. There was a giant of a man standing beside them. He had a thick black beard and his broad face looked fierce. With his abundance of muscles, she assumed he was a hired hand. Her husband-to-be would need help with a ranch as large as the one he described.

"Adam must have sent you," she said to him with a nod.

The man didn't deny it.

Now that she was steadier on her feet, Annabelle told herself Adam probably meant well by sending someone else to meet her. The train ride had been tiring. Maybe he thought she would want to shake some of the train soot out of her skirt before meeting him. Besides, she wouldn't mind learning a few more things about her future husband before she stood next to him. They'd have more to converse about that way. Her cousin's wife had reminded her before she left that Annabelle would not have to worry about her shyness if she remembered that men liked to talk about themselves.

She felt a tug on her dress.

"You wore your hat," Eliza said as she gazed up at her intently, her small fist clutching at the material in Annabelle's skirt.

She nodded. She'd never owned such an elaborate hat before. It had belonged to her cousin's wife, but she had lent it to Annabelle to have her photograph taken for the matrimonial ad. When the response came from Adam so quickly and with such a nice compliment about the hat, the other woman decided to give it to her. The kindness of the gesture had been touching as they both knew neither of them had money for another hat like that.

"Excuse us, ma'am," the man said, as he reached down and uncurled the girl's hand from the material in her dress. He looked like he wanted to snatch both children back from her embrace.

Annabelle tried to summon a smile for him. She told herself she had nothing to fear. Adam would not send anyone dangerous to meet her. Although, she admitted, this man was so tall and strong that he looked uncivilized. His blue eyes were a little startling, too. She'd never met anyone like him back in Connecticut, except for her father. And even he had not been as imposing as this. She was certainly grateful she didn't have to marry a man like him. She felt a flutter around her heart at the thought. Which surprised her until she realized it must be from the cold.

"I'm Gabe Stone, Adam's older brother," the man said then. She barely had time to notice that his voice had a nice lilt to it when he added in a more serious tone, "I'm afraid I have some disappointing news for you."

"Oh." Annabelle's nerve faltered. Maybe the flutter meant something else altogether. Half of her might have known something would happen. "What's wrong?"

She waited, but he didn't say any more.

She had prayed many times on the train journey here, as much to calm her nerves as to prepare herself for meeting her husband for the first time. It had been hard for her to trust God to take care of her after the fire, but she tried. She thought her prayers had been answered when Adam proposed. He seemed to be the perfect mate for her since he understood how her injuries limited her ability to do heavy work. When he confessed he wasn't a tall man, she'd also been grateful God had understood about her fears of large men.

"Maybe we should sit down somewhere," the man in front of her finally muttered.

She looked around and didn't see any benches on the platform. They were standing on boards of raw lumber and the wood frame depot beside them was new, too. She'd heard the railroad had just come to this town a year or so ago. People were standing around in clusters or moving their trunks away from the pile of luggage that had been carried off the train.

"Did something happen?" Annabelle whispered

when she couldn't wait any longer. She instinctively reached up to touch the golden locket around her neck. It had belonged to the mother she barely remembered and she was in the habit of wearing it even while she slept. It was the one thing that had survived the fire with her. "Is Adam hurt?"

The man stepped closer and held her elbow like he thought she might need steadying.

"No, Adam's fine."

"Oh, thanks be to God." She glanced upward. "Has he—" She looked back down and then stopped. She wasn't going to ask this man if Adam had changed his mind. Besides, it had to be something else. Surely Adam would not send a man like this to inform her if he decided not to marry her. A gentleman would explain something like that himself.

"Is he at his ranch?" she asked, suddenly remembering. "I understand if he needs to be there for the cattle."

She did not intend to be a demanding wife. Not that she needed to explain herself.

Gabe looked a little stunned at her remarks. "Cattle?"

She nodded. "I know how much work a whole herd can be. I think he said he had a hundred of them. Beautiful, fat cattle. But I suppose you know all about them."

The man was silent.

"You can wait with us for Pa," Daniel spoke then, his words rushing out as though he wanted to get all of them finished before something stopped him. He ended with a nervous glance at Gabe that would or-dinarily make Annabelle say something, but the little girl had taken a tiny step closer.

"It's almost Christmas," Eliza added in a whisper.

Annabelle knelt down to the two children. They both looked so solemn and wistful.

"Pa will be back soon," Daniel said, his eyes plead-ing with her. "I know he will."

She looked up at Gabe, trying to remember what Adam had said about him. She did recall him mention-ing that they were staying with his brother for a few weeks in—what was it that he called it?

"I'd be happy to help you in your store," Annabelle said as she remembered. It was some kind of a trad-ing post Adam had said. A frontier store for soldiers and, before that, Indians. She straightened up. "I used to help my father in a general store he owned until it burned down." She paused and then hurried on. "Adam told me you had an establishment outside of Miles City in a place called Dry Creek."

A man as grim as this one probably desperately needed help in his business, she thought. He might not realize how unsettling he seemed when he had that dark look on his face. People would be afraid of him. Even her father, with all his temper in private, had learned to be cordial to strangers in hopes they'd become customers.

Gabe finally shook his head. "Well, I wouldn't call it an establishment."

He didn't say anything more, but he had a hand on

each of the children's heads. It looked like he was comforting them. Then she noticed the snow was thicker than it had been. She looked at the railroad tracks and they were already white. No one would even know a train had stopped here.

Annabelle suddenly realized that, if she didn't go with the children, she would need to take a room at a hotel. She remembered Adam saying the town did have one. She looked around, but couldn't see the main part of the town from here. The railroad depot blocked her view. She had a little money, the amount she had received from selling the land that her father's store had sat upon, but the only offer she'd had for the property had been very low. She'd spent some money for her silk dress and a few Christmas presents. Annabelle doubted she'd have money for more than a week in a hotel and no one had mentioned how long Adam would be gone.

"I would be happy to stay with you and wait for your father," Annabelle said to the boy and then looked up at the man. "If that is all right with you, of course."

The man looked around like he hoped to see someone appear, but then he turned back to her.

"I could pay for a night or two in the Grand," Gabe said, the furrow in his forehead again.

His voice trailed off and he just looked at her.

"Adam can pay me back if that suits you better," he added when she didn't say anything.

She wondered what was best to do. The very name of the place sounded expensive. She didn't relish the endless hours spent alone in a hotel with the storm outside, either. And, as generous as Adam promised to be in his letters, she hated to meet her fiancé with a bill in hand.

"Christmas is coming," Eliza whispered. "You need to be with us at Christmas. Pa said."

Everyone was silent at that.

"You're right," Annabelle finally said. "Since we're to be family soon, I think it will be all right if I stay with you."

Christina had told her that many mail-order brides married hours after they arrived at their destination because of the distance of some of the ranches from preachers. Annabelle wasn't sure she would have been ready to say her marriage vows when she stepped off the train, but Adam obviously intended for her to wait with his brother and children. After all, he had sent them to meet her.

"I suppose you're tired," the man said then.

She nodded in relief. "And I'm sure there are things that need to be done to get ready for Christmas." She looked down at the children and smiled. "Your father said he wanted this to be a special one for both of you. I've hosted many a holiday meal so I'll do my best."

The little girl let out a sigh and whispered, "Christmas."

The man looked embarrassed. "We don't have anything fancy for guests when it comes to sleeping or anything."

"I can stay in the store if you have a cot," she offered. She had to be flexible now that she was out in the territories. She wondered if the poor man even had a proper house. It was unlikely he had a home as nice as Adam's. Her future husband had spent a whole paragraph in one of his letters telling her about the white linen curtains in the parlor of his ranch house.

"I couldn't let you do that." Gabe looked down and his face was grim.

She suddenly realized he wasn't just being polite—that he was worried about something else—and she bristled. "I assure you that I'm honest."

It was one thing for her to be hesitant about him, she thought, but surely he didn't suspect her of criminal tendencies. She'd poured out her heart to his brother in the letters she sent and Adam would have never asked her to be his wife if she were some unsavory sort of person.

"I didn't mean—" Gabe looked up in surprise and then reached up to brush the snow off his hair. "I'm sure you are honest. I meant I'll sleep in the storeroom. There's a strong lock on the door between the two if you're nervous. Like I said, the living quarters aren't much, but they're warmer than the rest of the place."

It wasn't a cordial invitation, but he did nod toward the pile of luggage that had been loaded off the train. "Which one is yours?"

"The brown one," she said and pointed to the well-worn valise. She didn't have much in it and she half expected him to comment on that, but he just walked over and picked it up, swinging it over his shoulder like it was empty.

She lifted her head high. Adam had promised to buy her a few new dresses. He might be gone away on some kind of business, but he would be back soon. After all, his children were expecting him. And Christmas was coming.

That's it, she thought to herself in relief. Adam must be away buying the children their Christmas presents. That's why everything his brother said seemed so guarded. The bearded man didn't look like he cared about Christmas secrets, but he must. And Adam was a thoughtful father for wanting his children to have a wonderful holiday.

She glanced sideways at the man who walked beside her. When she stood next to him, she realized he was taller and broader than her father had been. She knew it was unreasonable to believe that all large men were mean-spirited, but she still felt cautious.

Gabe seemed nice enough, but she hoped he didn't plan to live with them once she and Adam were married. She would be happy to leave the man's store and move out to the ranch. She didn't know much about ranching, but from Adam's descriptions she could almost picture the herd of cattle on the green prairie and the cozy ranch house with the rockers on the covered porch. It all sounded very peaceful. She decided Gabe must be jealous of his brother. That's why he looked so uncomfortable when talking about Adam's ranch. That trading post of his didn't sound like much.

Well, it didn't matter if Adam and Gabe didn't get along. Brothers had had trouble since Cain and Abel. She wouldn't let that spoil her anticipation. After Christmas, she thought to herself, she and Adam would get married and they could move out to his place. She'd do everything she could to see they were happy together. She'd remember to work as hard as she was able and keep in mind that men liked peacocks and not barn hens. If she used a few tricks, she could be prettier. Christina had shown her a new hairstyle on the train. And, she was grateful for the beautiful hat she wore. No one could accuse her of being drab when she was wearing that headpiece.

She glanced over at Adam's brother again and wondered if he thought she was colorful enough. Not that it mattered, she thought, as she felt that odd flutter near her heart again. She pulled her shawl tighter around her shoulders. She'd never been affected by the cold like this before, but that must be what was causing that flutter. She hadn't even met her handsome husband yet.

She looked at Gabe again. Yes, it was most unusual, she thought. There was nothing in the large man that resembled the picture she'd formed in her mind of her Adam. The brothers were not alike and she was grateful for that. She couldn't wait to meet Adam.

Chapter Two

Gabe decided he was in more trouble than he'd been when he was waiting for the train to come. He didn't want to disappoint Annabelle so he wasn't going to tell her about the note—which meant he had to find his brother as soon as he could and make him come back to his bride. He could see by the look in Annabelle's eyes that she was half in love with Adam already and love was not something to be sent away. His brother should know that.

Gabe adjusted the valise in his arms and motioned for the children to follow him as he began to walk to the edge of the platform. He'd do what he could to bring happiness to his brother.

"Ready?" Gabe turned to ask.

Three heads nodded.

When Gabe stepped off the platform, the gust hit him full force. The only reason there was no dust blowing was because the rain a month ago had packed

down the roads. Specks of ice and snow flew in his
face and he was grateful for the thick wool shirt he
wore. He reached up and raised his collar to protect
his neck. A horse nickered farther down the street and
Gabe looked over to see a man urging his buggy into
an alley. The street was empty except for that—unless
he counted the three people wrapped in black cloaks
who were bending in the wind as they slowly made
their way toward the Broadwater, Bubble and Company Mercantile. They looked like crows since they
all had their heads down and the sides of their cloaks
billowed out like wings.

"Let me help," Gabe said as he turned to the children. Annabelle had already gathered the little ones
to her and they were standing on the edge of the platform swaying like weeds in a storm. They weren't
even in the full wind yet, though. Gabe reached up to
help each one down and then stayed close. The children attached themselves to Annabelle again and he
put his arm around her shoulders to steady everyone.

Gabe felt Annabelle stiffen and she glanced up at
him as though to say something. He supposed that
putting his arm around her was inappropriate from
her point of view. Before she could speak though an
even stronger blast of air hit and sent her frothy hat
spinning upward.

"I'll get it," Gabe yelled as he stretched upward to
grab the hat. If he'd been an inch shorter, he'd have
missed it. He tried not to get tangled in the pink net-
ting as he offered it back to her with one hand. When

she took it, she nodded to him so he hoped that meant she understood the rules of politeness were different out West, especially in this kind of situation.

Gabe reached down and lifted Eliza up to his chest. His niece buried her head in the curve of his neck and he risked stepping close to Annabelle once again. Daniel was on the other side of her and the coat weighed him down enough so he was able to withstand the wind. When Gabe put his arm around Annabelle this time, she didn't resist.

The sky grew darker and the air more frigid as they slowly walked across the street. What they were experiencing was a warning more than a storm, though, Gabe finally decided. It would likely be another hour before the snow started to fall in earnest. The air wasn't heavy enough yet and the wind would likely calm down as it grew warmer. They would have time to get home before the worst of it arrived.

With his arm still around Annabelle, Gabe led the way toward the open wagon that he'd left beside the mercantile. Fortunately, the store kept the wind away from the horses so they looked passably content to stand where he'd tied them. A small section of boardwalk led to the door of the store and large windows allowed anyone going by to see the displays.

"Oh, my." Annabelle stepped in front of the side window that was filled with saddlebags and riding chaps. The wind didn't bother anyone that close to the building so Gabe stopped, too. She was studying the merchandise carefully and he was holding his breath.

He hadn't told anyone that he was the one making the leather goods for the mercantile. Until now, he hadn't cared what anyone thought of them, either. They either bought them or they didn't. As a boy, after Adam had been sent away, Gabe continued going with his father into the mountains to work their traplines. His father didn't talk much so Gabe had worked out his loneliness with a rawhide mallet, an old stub knife and some pieces of tanned leather. Over the years, he had made enough saddlebags to outfit an army. Recently he'd started fashioning his own designs on riding chaps and knife sheaths.

Annabelle kept looking through the window, but she didn't say anything more.

Gabe decided she was taking too much time. "What's wrong?"

He supposed the wildlife pictures he'd carved into the leather were too primitive for her. She'd probably rather have flowers like the ones she had on her hat instead of a mountain lion caught in midjump. A flower wouldn't sell a saddlebag, though, not if a man were buying it.

"Nothing," Annabelle said as she stepped closer to the window. "I just thought these bags looked familiar. My father sold some with a bear tooled on the front of them like the one in the back there. Some famous artist did them."

As far as Gabe knew, his work had never made it back East, but sometimes a traveling peddler bought a few dozen so it was possible a saddlebag had got-

ten back to a store in Connecticut. No one called him
an artist, but he felt a moment's pride believing Annabelle appreciated what he'd made. Then she looked
beyond the leather goods into the interior of the mercantile and she seemed even more alert, like she was
searching for something.

"We can go inside," he said. He should have realized that any woman would want some things at the
end of a journey like hers. "I have to pick up my order
anyway."

Annabelle nodded and put her head back down.

Gabe was the first to reach the door and he opened
it just enough for Eliza to slip inside. Then he helped
Annabelle and Daniel enter. Gabe closed the door behind himself, feeling relief at the sudden warmth. The
rich smell of spices surrounded him as he glanced at
the bolts of fabric on a nearby table. The overcast sky
outside meant the light was dim inside the store, but
the goods on shelves and table were plainly visible. He
expected Annabelle to step over and touch the cloth.
All of the women were drawn to the silk even if they
could only afford gingham and he already knew she
was accustomed to silk from the dress she was wearing
now. She was looking around at everything as though
making some kind of an assessment of the whole place.

Gabe supposed the store was lacking compared to
the one her father had owned. He tried to see the large
room through her eyes. Things might seem jumbled
to her. The spools of thread sat on top of a stack of
canned goods with tooth powder next to them. An

open barrel of pickles stood by itself in the corner next
to a scarred wooden stool that held a few old news-
papers that, though used, were still for sale. People
were most often in a hurry to buy what they needed
in this store and they didn't require it be neatly dis-
played on shelves.

"Some blizzard we've got starting out there." The
clerk turned from behind the dark wood counter and
pushed up his green eyeshade. He seemed to suddenly
recognize Gabe. "Oh, Mr. Stone. You're back."

Gabe nodded. His brother had told him once that
the brass trim on the counters here was as bright as
anything a body would find on the East Coast and that
made Gabe feel good. The clerk, a short bald man, his
black suspenders crossing over a rumpled white shirt,
might not be everyone's idea of a gentleman's clerk,
but he had gladly taken Gabe's order earlier in the day
for some dried beans and a slab of bacon.

"I've got your things by the back door," the man
added, sounding harried. "If you just give me a minute, I'll load them for you."

The clerk pushed his eyeshade back down and rolled
his eyes to the side, indicating his attention was required elsewhere.

Gabe turned and saw the three people in the black
cloaks. Their wool garments were damp and they were
huddled together looking down at something in the
glass case. Not too many people shopped at that particular case; it was where the gold watches were kept,

safely locked away so temptation couldn't overtake anyone of humble means.

"I'll be right there." The clerk pulled a brass key ring from under the counter and walked over to wait on the three customers. "You'll find those are very rare."

One figure straightened up and Gabe noticed the purple feathers in the woman's hat. He'd seen those silly things bob in church too many Sundays not to recognize them.

"Mrs. Ida Baker," he muttered by way of greeting and the woman turned toward him slightly. The middle-aged woman, wife of one of the railroad men, was a little stout, but her face had strong features. She'd look fine, Gabe thought, if she'd get rid of those feathers in her hat. And that self-righteous expression on her face.

The older woman didn't acknowledge his greeting, but her eyes narrowed so he knew she'd heard him and recognized him from the times he'd sat in the pew behind her. As far as he could tell, Ida Baker was the woman stirring up all of the gossip about Adam and the children. After he'd heard her say something about the children benefitting from adoption, Gabe had made a point of attending church and taking Daniel and Eliza with him. His mother had taught him about God and, to his surprise, he found his childhood faith slowly rekindled as he listened to the preacher.

"Ohhh." A sigh came from down around Gabe's kneecaps and he looked down to see a look of sweet adoration on Eliza's face.

The girl pointed at the object she found fascinating. "Pretty."

Gabe started to say something about how expensive the items in that case were, but, while listening to the preacher of late, Gabe had come to understand that even children needed hope.

"These decorations are handblown glass from Germany," the clerk said as he lifted a golden pear out of the display case and held it up so everyone could see it. "Even one of these on a Christmas tree makes a whole house shine."

The clerk had his eye on Mrs. Baker when he was talking, but she didn't seem moved. That didn't stop him, though, and he turned the pear until he found a bit of sunshine. The light cast golden flecks everywhere as it passed through the ornament. "See?"

Mrs. Baker looked more interested then. "If it were more than just a simple pear, I might buy one. But my husband promised to bring me some glass berries from back East. They're in clusters and are supposed to shine even on a dark day. These kinds of ornaments are popular in all of the better homes back there."

"My father used to sell them in his store," Annabelle said softly, still standing beside Gabe, but craning her head to look around him to the other woman.

Gabe resisted the urge to step forward and shield Annabelle from the other woman.

As it was, Mrs. Baker met his expectations as she frowned slightly at Annabelle, no doubt wondering if she knew her. If it wasn't for the rose hat that Annabelle wore, Gabe was sure Mrs. Baker wouldn't even give her that much attention.

Gabe was getting ready to make an introduction when the other woman standing beside Mrs. Baker sighed just like Eliza had. She had a knit scarf wrapped around her head as if she had an earache.

"One of my friends in Philadelphia has a pear like that," the woman said, her voice wistful as she looked up at the clerk. "I haven't seen them in any of the shops this year. They are most beautiful."

"I am afraid they're too dear for us still." The man spoke then. His words were low, not meant to be heard by the others. Gabe assumed he was the woman's husband since he gave her a small smile. "Besides, Christmas isn't about a decorated tree. We both know that."

"Oh, but surely for this year." Mrs. Baker turned to the man. "A pear like that can make a home feel special for the holidays. And with your loss, I'm sure you can make an exception."

"A holiday ornament won't bring our little Mary back," the man said.

Everyone was silent at that and, after a few minutes, the clerk set the pear down on the counter.

Gabe took a step forward and, when Annabelle followed him, the clerk seemed to suddenly sense a new prospect. "Oh, I say. Would the two of you be interested in the pear?"

Mrs. Baker snorted. "That's hardly the kind of thing the Stone family would want. They don't even have a house to keep it in."

Gabe turned his back. He might have been raised in the mountains, but his mother had taught him to be polite to all women. He wished he could forget that for a few moments, but he knew he'd regret saying anything to Mrs. Baker. He'd just have to ignore the feathered woman.

He looked down at Annabelle instead. "Do you need anything before we head out?"

Eliza had taken hold of the leg of his pants and Daniel was standing on the other side of Annabelle.

She looked undecided for a moment, but then shook her head. "I'll wait for Adam to get here."

For some reason, that annoyed Gabe more than it should. Maybe because he had been proud when the clerk assumed Annabelle was with him. Besides, he had enough money for whatever little thing a woman would want. She didn't need to wait for his brother.

"I have a good price on hairpins," the clerk said with a helpful smile, looking at them as though trying to decide what the relationship was between them now that Adam had been mentioned. Only the owner of the mercantile talked with Gabe about his leatherwork, but Gabe saw the clerk often enough that the man knew that neither he nor Adam had a wife.

Gabe looked down and saw that the wind had blown Annabelle's chestnut-colored hair this way and that until it tumbled around her face. It had also brought a pale pink color to her cheeks. Only a few strands of her hair were still caught in the gathering she'd made at the nape of her neck. She was holding her bedraggled hat, but she put the other hand up to her head in dismay. He could see her feeling around for those pins. He watched long enough to realize she wasn't finding them.

The three other people had stopped looking at anything in the store, but were talking quietly to each other so Gabe figured it was safe to continue ignoring them.

"We'll take a dozen." He made a guess; she had nice, thick hair. It had a shine to it that he liked, too. He had to stop himself from wondering what it would feel like to bury his hands in it. But that was probably only the cold outside affecting his senses and giving him strange impulses.

"They're good quality pins," the clerk assured him with an eager smile now that at least some sale was possible. "Came all the way from France. You won't be sorry."

Annabelle gasped in horror. "From France!"

Gabe thought he also heard another gasp from Mrs. Baker's lips, but he refused to look over at the woman again to see. Instead, he looked at Annabelle, who put a hand to her throat and turned to him.

"I can't afford something like that," she said. "Not when I lose the stray pin here and there. I always buy the cheapest pins so that when they fall out I can replace them."

"And I expect those pins don't keep your hair in place as well as they ought," the clerk interjected. "Hair like yours does best with a quality pin."

"Well, I—" Annabelle stammered, her cheeks even pinker as she put her hand up to her hair and tried to tuck the strands into their former shape. "I just can't afford them."

"I'll make them an early Christmas present," Gabe said without thinking. She had such beautiful hair; he didn't want her to be distressed over it.

"That's not necessary," Annabelle said, her cheeks fully flushed by now.

"Just add them to my account, please," he said.

Mrs. Baker and her friends were looking at him and he'd just as soon get his order finished.

Unfortunately, the clerk was a better salesman than Gabe had figured he was. He had learned to tell when a man might want to please a woman, and Gabe didn't want the man to suggest something more. There would be no impressing Annabelle anyway. If he couldn't convince his brother to return, Annabelle wasn't going to want to have much to do with him, either. A few French pins wouldn't change that.

"I'll maybe get some molasses, too," he informed the clerk to take everyone's minds off the hairpins. "And a half-dozen of those canned peaches you keep. Some cornmeal and flour. Might as well add salt and some cinnamon. Dried apples, too, and some lard."

"Anything else we need?" Gabe asked as he paused long enough to look down at Annabelle.

She shook her head. Her color had gone back to normal.

But Gabe kept going. "Sugar, of course. Some baking powder and one of those fine hanging hams you keep in the back. Make that two of the hams and some eggs. A bag of good coffee, too." He thought of Daniel and Eliza. "And a few tablets of paper and two pencils."

He looked down beside him and saw that the children weren't there. So he leaned closer to the clerk and whispered. "As long as we're at it, put in a handful of lemon drops for the children. And a good-sized bag of the peanuts you keep on the shelf."

Gabe stopped before he bought everything in the store. He had heard the shuffling of shoes as he'd been putting in his order so he knew Mrs. Baker and the couple had moved to look at something else. He thought, from the sounds of their voices, that it was a new lantern that had their attention. Fortunately, he had two good ones back at the post.

The clerk turned around and started pulling sacks off the shelves. "Your brother stopped by just after I opened this morning," he said with his back to Gabe. "Got some supplies—green coffee and beans mostly. A bit of bacon and some of those peaches you like. Signed your name for it. Traveling supplies. He said you'd told him to do it."

Gabe didn't get a chance to answer before he heard a woman's voice coming from behind him.

"Isn't she adorable?"

Gabe looked over his shoulder in time to see Mrs. Baker bending down to Eliza. When she tilted her head, Eliza looked up at that feather in her purple hat as though fascinated by it.

"Pretty," Eliza said as she reached for the decoration.

"Oh, dear," Mrs. Baker said with a laugh as she straightened up, taking the feather with her. "Isn't she just precious? I'm so glad we could see her."

The elderly couple was beaming at Eliza, too.

"She certainly is sweet," the wife said as she put a gloved hand out to touch Eliza's cheek. "Perfect really. Our Mary would have wanted that feather, too. This little one reminds me so much of her, standing here like she is."

Gabe felt himself break out into a cold sweat and he walked over to the three of them. "Eliza's with me."

Then he took his niece by the hand and led her back to where Annabelle stood. The couple was still looking at Eliza, though. Their eyes might be uncertain, but they hadn't turned away.

"I'm her uncle," Gabe said, scowling at the older man. "Eliza's got a home."

"But not a father, apparently," Mrs. Baker said as she stepped forward, her dress rustling beneath the cloak as she moved. She put her hand to her throat, obviously trying to look sympathetic. "I heard the clerk say that the children's father had ridden through town this morning on his way to who-knows-where. How will you manage?"

"His name is Adam," Gabe said, not bothering to

hide his irritation. "Adam Stone. And we'll manage just fine. I can provide for the children."

"Well, be that as it may," Mrs. Baker said, her voice more strident, "they need a legal guardian and, if their father is away, they might have a problem. We don't know if he's ever coming back, now do we?"

"Hush," Gabe said as he glared at her before he looked down to Eliza.

Mrs. Baker pursed her lips and swished her skirts slightly.

"If you're so worried about my brother," Gabe looked up to her and said, "you should be praying for him, not working against him."

He might not have gone to church much since his mother had taught him about the Bible as a child, but he did know some things.

"Well, I never." Mrs. Baker drew herself up indignantly.

Gabe didn't have time to answer her.

Instead, he glanced down to assure his niece. "Don't worry. Your pa's coming back." She looked at him with a tear forming in her eye and he picked her up and settled her against his chest. This time she leaned into him as he patted her.

Eliza was still trembling so he bent close to whisper in her ear. "I'm going to go and get him. Don't you cry. I know just how to find him. No one can hide from your uncle Gabe."

Eliza nodded her head against him and she seemed to relax. He felt good that she trusted him to do what she needed. He hoped he wasn't promising too much. He figured Adam could be found at the biggest poker game around. He'd drink himself senseless and then become convinced he could win his fortune on the turn of a card. If Gabe waited until the game was over, his brother would be easy enough to lead home.

It wasn't until he had patted Eliza a couple of more times that Gabe realized the girl wasn't the only one who might be worried after hearing Mrs. Baker's words. He looked over at Annabelle and saw that her face had gone white.

"He left?" She stood straighter and asked Mrs. Baker.

Something about Annabelle's voice must have made the other woman cautious. It was likely one thing to terrify a child, another to face an adult.

"Do you know him, dear?" the older woman murmured, her voice softer than it had been.

"I'm his bride-to-be," Annabelle answered bleakly.

"Oh," Mrs. Baker said in surprise. The feather on her hat bobbed. "Oh."

Gabe thought things couldn't get any worse and then Annabelle looked up at him. "Adam didn't tell anyone he was getting married?"

Gabe glanced over at the counter. He wished he could climb behind it and hide. "Well, I'm sure he told—" Gabe cleared his throat. "That is—my brother was looking forward to—"

He stopped before he outright lied. Adam had

seemed resigned to the marriage, but Gabe doubted it would be any comfort to Annabelle if he said that.

Mrs. Baker stepped closer. "So you'd be the children's mother, then?"

Annabelle nodded.

"*If* the marriage happens," Mrs. Baker added, her eyes squinting slightly as she studied Annabelle. Strangely enough, her tone wasn't unkind even with the words she was saying. "From what I know of Adam, you don't seem the kind of woman he would seek out. He likes *those* other kind of women, you know."

Gabe wondered if things could get any worse.

"Adam is a gentleman," Annabelle replied, her tone icy by now.

Mrs. Baker waved her hand around. "Maybe he was at one time, but surely you can't think he is now."

Gabe didn't like the expression on Annabelle's face. She looked frozen.

"Adam is a good man. He's just troubled." Gabe tightened his arm around Eliza. It was time for some plain speaking. "And the children still have me. There's no call for an adoption."

"Well, really," Mrs. Baker said in exasperation, turning from Annabelle to him. "You're a man—who lives up in those mountains." She gave another vague wave to the west. "You can't expect a judge to believe you know more about raising a little girl than my sister Ethel here?"

Her sister? Gabe thought. That couldn't be good.

"I live here now," he said firmly. He hadn't stood up in church and made any announcements, but he knew she had seen him sitting there all those Sundays. He'd had his fill of trapping and liked his work with leather. He intended to make a home here. His heart sank when he realized Mrs. Baker might not care where he lived or what he did. She wanted the girl for her relatives. To replace their Mary.

He looked over at the sister and his gaze softened. "I'm sorry about your daughter."

"Granddaughter," the woman whispered.

"Granddaughter, then," Gabe repeated. "But I'm going to keep the children with me until Adam is better. I live in the trading post my father used to run."

She nodded at him, but didn't say anything.

"See, what kind of a life—" Mrs. Baker shook her head as she turned to her sister. "A trading post! That poor girl needs a home. Some place warm, filled with love and laughter." She turned back to Gabe. "Ethel here makes the most wonderful cookies. Why, I doubt you even have a doll for her."

Mrs. Baker gestured to the one sitting on the shelf behind her.

Gabe had been making Eliza a leather doll for Christmas, but he knew it didn't compare to the blond painted one on the shelf. That doll's red cotton dress made it look like a little girl's dream. He didn't even have a dress for the doll he was making. He'd planned to cut off a corner of the wool blanket he used on his bed so Eliza could wrap her doll in that.

He could see Mrs. Baker making the same arguments to a territorial judge. One of them usually came to Miles City, too, to spend the holiday with family. Gabe remembered suddenly that he had heard somewhere the man was a cousin to Mrs. Baker.

"I have a good home for the children," Gabe argued in desperation, realizing no one had mentioned his nephew. They must only want Eliza. It would be the separation of him and Adam all over again. No cookies or dolls could make up for losing a brother.

"Really?" Mrs. Baker's voice challenged him.

"We're going to have a Christmas party," Gabe added. He wasn't going to let the children be separated. Before he lost his nerve, he jumped off the cliff completely. "You're invited."

Mrs. Baker was speechless.

He turned to the couple. "You, too, of course. Please join us."

Gabe had faced down a wounded bear a few winters ago along the tree line heading up to the Rockies. He knew what it was to bluff when a man was in a fight to survive. He figured unless he gave some invitation like this, Mrs. Baker would decide to visit on her own. She'd even bring the judge along. She'd look for every reason to say he wasn't providing a good home for the children. But, if she thought he really had an adequate place, she wouldn't bother. Everyone was busy close to the holidays.

"What time?" Mrs. Baker asked then.

Gabe kept his expression neutral. The secret to

a successful bluff was to not flinch. "Five o'clock, Christmas Eve. Just before dark."

He congratulated himself on making the hour late. Most people preferred to be snug at home by then.

"I'll be there," Mrs. Baker said. "My husband is on a business trip and won't be home until after Christmas."

"We'd love to come, too," the wife of the couple said with a look at Eliza. "It's been a long time since we've spent Christmas Eve with a little girl. We lost our own Mary about this same time last year."

Gabe figured he was fortunate he'd survived his encounter with that bear. His instincts were off. At least, this certainly wasn't going the way he had expected.

Just then there was the tinkling sound of fine glass breaking. Gabe had an ominous feeling as he turned around and saw Daniel standing by the far counter, a stricken look on his face and the sleeve of his coat trailing over the top of the now-bare display case.

"I only wanted to touch it," the boy said, his voice trembling, as he looked down at the shattered pear ornament.

"Look what he's done!" Mrs. Baker said as she turned to Gabe. "That boy needs a good whipping. Someone needs to teach him how to behave."

"Daniel is a fine boy," Gabe answered back firmly and was rewarded when the boy lifted his eyes to him in gratitude.

"Nonsense—he's running wild," Mrs. Baker retorted. With that, she put her nose in the air. "You'll have to pay for that, you know."

Gabe heard the catch in Daniel's breath.

"I planned to buy both of the pears anyway," Gabe said calmly. And the thought had run through his mind.

"Don't be ridiculous." Mrs. Baker turned to scold him, her face twisted in disgust. "What would you do with an ornament like that anyway?"

"We'll put it on the Christmas tree in our home," Gabe assured her. "Like every other fine family this holiday season that owns one of them."

"Well, I never," the older woman said with a sniff as she turned to leave. She led the couple over to the door and out of the store.

Gabe watched them go, wondering how he was going to transform his trading post into a suitable home in three days. Then he remembered that neither Mrs. Baker nor her relatives knew where he lived.

He breathed a sigh of relief. Some of the soldiers at the fort would have been around here long enough to remember his father's trading post, but Mrs. Baker wasn't likely to be friendly with any of them. He and the children were safe. All they needed to do was to stay away from Miles City until all of Mrs. Baker's family left town, especially the judge.

He looked up when he heard the door open again. The gentleman had returned.

"That's the old trading post the men used from Fort Keogh, isn't it?" the man asked.

Gabe nodded.

"Good. Our son—Mary's father—was assigned to the fort some years ago. I know just where it is."

Gabe almost wished that bear had gotten him. How was he going to put on a Christmas party?

He turned back to the clerk and pulled a gold coin from his pocket. "This should cover both pears."

The clerk's eyes grew big. "You don't have to buy the second one. Don't let Mrs. Baker give you a hard time. I'll talk to the owner about the broken one, too. It was an accident. We've had those pears on the shelf for three years now. The owners didn't think we'd ever sell them."

"I know. I still want the second one."

The clerk looked at him like he had lost his senses. First, French pins and then German fruit. Gabe didn't say anything, but he would spend every penny he had if it would make Daniel stop looking at the floor in shame and cause people like Mrs. Baker to think the children were safe in their uncle's hands.

He looked over at Annabelle. He'd spend even more to see her eyes smile at Christmas.

Snow covered the ground beneath the moving wagon as Annabelle sat on the front seat. Everything around them was white, too, she admitted as she shifted on the wooden planks, trying to keep the buffalo robe from touching her too closely. She had no idea what kind of vermin were crawling around on the hide even though the children were snuggly wrapped in another such robe behind her and they didn't seem bothered by anything. She had been eager to leave the mercantile and now she was regretting it. Being humiliated was actually slightly more bearable than freezing to death, she realized.

"You could have told me Adam had left," she complained softly to Gabe as she shifted the robe closer. Her hair felt like it was freezing solid to her scalp. At least, she had been able to slip her hat under the wool blanket that Gabe had put over the supplies in the back of the wagon. The poor headpiece was probably warmer now than she was although she couldn't answer for its shape after being whipped around in the wind the way it had been.

"Wouldn't have made any difference," Gabe said, sparing her a glance before turning to stare at the backs of the horses as they plodded through the gathering snow.

"Well, it would have made a difference to me," she said tartly, watching as her breath left in white puffs.

He didn't respond to that and it was just as well, she told herself. Really, what would she have done if she had known? She supposed she could have asked if there was a position open at the mercantile, but she doubted the present clerk would be willing to tell her if there was one even though she surely could improve on the arrangement of the goods they had. She had done very well in her father's store.

Unfortunately, she didn't have the skills for any other kind of a job that might be available in a frontier town. And, as she'd figured out earlier, she didn't have enough money to stay at a hotel until she figured out where to go next. She supposed her cousin would send her some money, but he had little to spare and she hated to ask it of him.

"I'll bring Adam back," Gabe said then. "Don't you worry. He'll do right by you."

Annabelle wondered if that was supposed to be comforting. She had begun to hope for a declaration of love from her husband-to-be. She supposed that was foolish, but she had anyway. Giggling with Christina on the way here on the train had given rise to all kinds of girlish dreams.

Now all of the things her father had said about her came back to haunt her. At her age, she should know better than to dream of romance. Then she straightened her shoulders as best she could. She might be a drab woman, she told herself, but there was no reason a man needed to be *forced* to wed her. She could just see Gabe towering over her and Adam as they stood in front of a preacher. That would be ten times worse than anything her father had ever done.

She looked at the man now and was struck at how fiercely he was frowning as he faced into the snow. Flakes were falling on his dark beard and gave a little sparkle even in the failing light. She doubted he was upset about her, though. Maybe his face just naturally looked gruff no matter what he was feeling.

"I didn't understand why Mrs. Baker was so interested in Eliza," she said then, telling herself she needed to get over her nervousness around the man even if he was disgruntled.

"She wants her sister to adopt the girl," Gabe said, his voice low so it wouldn't reach the children behind them.

"But she can't do that," Annabelle protested as she forgot her own problems. No wonder the man was surly. "Adam is her father."

Her mother had died, too, and Annabelle's father had never been particularly nice to her, but no one ever thought of taking her away from him. People just didn't do that kind of thing.

"The laws are different out here," Gabe said. "And Mrs. Baker has some sway with a territorial judge. She doesn't think a father like Adam is adequate. Or an uncle apparently."

"That's ridiculous." Families belonged together, she told herself, even if there weren't two parents left.

"She might get the judge to agree with her," Gabe added bleakly. "A girl Eliza's age could sure use a mother. You know, for dolls and cookies and those kinds of things. I don't even know how to braid her hair very well. I try, but it turns out stiff. And she wants curls."

"I can teach you to curl her hair." Annabelle put her hand on his arm. She suddenly had that fluttery feeling around her heart again. She wondered if it was stress. She'd have to write Christina and ask her about it. Maybe there was a change in altitude or something that she was unaware of.

The man's face was still in shadows, but she could see the light in his dark blue eyes as he looked at her.

"Thank you," Gabe said, smiling. "I'd appreciate that."

"You're welcome," Annabelle replied a little shyly. "I'll teach you how to make some cookies, too. Anyone can make sugar cookies and, if you sprinkle a little cinnamon on them, too, they're really good."

There didn't seem to be anything else to say so she put the buffalo robe up higher to try and cover her neck. One good thing about this kind of weather, she told herself, was that any flea would surely freeze to death before it could bite her.

She glanced sideways at the man again. Somehow sitting this close to him didn't make her as nervous anymore. A mean-spirited man wouldn't worry about a little girl's hair, would he? Her father certainly never had. She decided as she stole glances at his face that he might not be as fierce as she had thought at first, either. She really had no objection to his face, she decided. In fact, it was kind of nice.

Annabelle must have closed her eyes with that thought, because she found herself startled awake when the horses stopped.

"Oh, dear," she murmured as she tried to sit upright and found she couldn't.

She wondered what was wrong and then figured out that she was being held in place by the man's arm. To her dismay, she realized she must have been using his shoulder for a pillow, with the buffalo robe tucked around her to keep the snow off her hair. Even as a child, her father had never permitted her to fall asleep against him and to do so to a stranger was unthinkable. She looked up to see if he was angry. Her father would have been boiling by now.

"I'm sorry," she whispered as she moved her injured arm closer to her side. The cold was making it ache more than usual. The way the scar from the burns had healed made it hard for her to use that arm fully and it went stiff if she left it in the same position for long.

The snow was falling like a blanket around her and she tried to forget the soreness. The sun was setting and, while even white flakes were sprinkled on the man's beard, his face was mostly shadows. He didn't look upset. About ten feet in front of them, she saw a vague shape through the blizzard. It looked like the house had been built into the side of a small hillside. With snowdrifts on every side, the place looked more like a dumpling than a building.

"Easy," Gabe said then, his voice low and soothing as he pulled the horses to a stop. "Let me get these reins tied up and then we'll get you inside."

The heat rose up in Annabelle's face. She could still feel his muscles as he moved his other arm to take care of the reins. He was certainly very solid.

"Are you all right?" he asked.

"I don't know what came over me." She tried to keep the nervousness out of her voice. Her father only punished her more if she sounded weak.

"You were tired." Gabe tied the reins to a corner of the wagon. The horses stood in place.

"Still," she said, wondering if he was sincere. "A lady never forgets where she is."

She chanced another look at his face.

"I hope you won't mention it to Adam," she added, suddenly remembering who her intended husband was. "I know some men would be anxious about the virtue of their mail-order bride and—"

"Adam has more sense than that," Gabe said, his voice clipped, as he put his hand on the back of the seat and jumped off the wagon. "I'll only take a minute to carry the children inside then I'll be back for you."

"I can—" She started to slide across the wooden plank that served as a seat.

"No need," he said, his voice muffled as he lifted a child in each arm and turned toward the building.

She watched as Gabe opened a tall wooden door. Except for some square windows, fluffy snow covered the outside walls and smoothed the way back to the sloping hillside. Her cousin had cautioned her to expect unusual things out here in the territories, but she rather liked the snow. It seemed heavier than the flakes back in Connecticut, but surely that was just a fancy of hers.

A minute later, Gabe stepped outside of the structure and walked back to the wagon. He held his arms out to her. "Try to keep the buffalo robe around you. No need to get cold now that you're here."

Annabelle slid across to the edge of the bench, clutching the robe around her. "I can walk."

"No need," Gabe repeated as he scooped her up.

Before she could stop it, sudden panic raced through Annabelle. Sitting beside the man was one thing, but putting herself in his total control was another. She told herself the man meant no harm, but she couldn't stop the fear as he pulled her tight to his chest.

"What's wrong?" Gabe stood in front of the door and looked down at her. Snow was still falling and the only reason she saw the flakes was because they were so white.

It was almost dark and she knew he couldn't see the expression on her face.

"I'm fine." Or, she would be soon, she told herself.

"You're about ready to take off running away from me," he contradicted her. "I want to know what's wrong."

"Could we just go inside?" she asked. Her heart was beating like a bird's and she felt foolish.

"I hope I haven't given you any cause to be afraid of me," he said, his voice soft.

She didn't answer for a minute and he didn't move.

Finally, she said, "You just remind me of someone."

"Someone who hurt you?" His voice sounded out-raged.

She couldn't speak, but she did nod.

At least he started to move then. He pushed the door open with his shoulder and carried her inside. The man must have stirred the fire before he came for her because it was burning low and steady in a rock fireplace on the far wall. The children were huddled together, sitting on the floor in front of it. The light didn't reach the far corners of the room, but it did light up the front area.

Gabe carried her over to a crude wooden table and sat her on a bench beside it.

"It will be warm in a few minutes," he said as he sat down in front of her and picked up one of her feet.

She watched in astonishment as he removed her shoe and started to rub her foot.

"Whatever are you doing?" she asked, a squeak in her voice that she tried to still.

"I didn't realize until I started to carry you inside that your stockings are so thin." He reached for the other foot and started to unlace that shoe, too. "We need to get your feet warm. And you'll need thicker socks in this kind of weather."

"But—" Annabelle began and then gave up. She'd never had a man care about her feet before. If it weren't for the intelligence she had seen in his eyes earlier at the railroad station, she would wonder if he were one of those childlike giants she'd heard about, the ones who could lift up a horse but who still couldn't be taught to read or reason.

As he rubbed her feet, she began to relax. She could feel the warmth all the way up her legs. She heard the children talking with each other in front of the fire and she looked around.

"This was a store?" she asked. There was more

darkness than light in the room and she could barely make out the dimensions. She did notice some shelves that had been pushed against one wall along with a counter. A blanket covered a stack of something in one corner and several rifles hung in a rack along the wall closest to her. She could almost smell a pickle barrel, too, although she didn't see one.

"My father closed it up before he died," Gabe said. "Almost nine years ago now."

She nodded her head.

"He sold to the soldiers," Gabe added. "And, once in a while, to a few Indians. Saddles. Ammunition. Whiskey. Little things. Buttons even. He carried whatever he thought a man alone would need. The place was always open when we weren't out trapping."

They were silent for a few minutes after that. Annabelle felt herself growing more comfortable. The more heat in the room, the more drowsy she became.

"Who was he?" Gabe asked her suddenly. "The man who frightened you?"

"My father," she said and then tried to undo any harm she had done. "It was mostly discipline, though. He meant well."

Gabe grunted in disbelief. "Not if you're still afraid. Did he beat you?"

She didn't know how he had guessed, but she couldn't admit the truth. She wasn't even sure what was normal discipline from a father. The switches he had cut hurt as he whipped her, but it was his anger that scared her more.

No man wanted to marry a barn hen, though, she reminded herself. Adam might not like it if she flinched and was timid. She would have to be sure he didn't see her acting afraid. Then, even if Gabe did say something to his brother, Adam would shrug it off.

"I'm perfectly fine now." She forced herself to put some confidence in her voice as she stood up. "And I'd appreciate it if you don't mention anything about my father to Adam."

Gabe grunted, but then nodded.

She needed Adam to accept her. Even if he was not happy to marry her, she could work to make something good of their lives together. She looked over at the two children. For her sake and for them, she would make a family. What other choice did she have? She couldn't go back to her cousin.

"When are you going for Adam?" she asked Gabe as she took a tentative step toward the children.

He didn't answer for a minute. Then he said. "Probably in the morning."

She nodded.

"But right now, I need to step out and see that the horses are in their shed and have some oats," Gabe said as he started walking toward the door. "Then I'll see about getting you a pair of socks. They'll be too big, but your feet will just get cold again unless you have something. Your shoes need to dry out before you can wear them again."

She watched as Gabe disappeared out the door. Before she left Connecticut, her cousin's wife had told her that God would not test her beyond what she was able to endure. She needed to remember that. Gabe was going to be part of her family; she would grow accustomed to him. She waited a minute, but no flutter came and that made her nod in satisfaction. She had settled down. It must have been nerves.

She wondered if she'd feel anything at all when she met Adam. She had no doubt Gabe would find him and bring him back. Her hopes of romance were gone, though. How could she love someone who was reluctant to marry her?

Lord, guide me, she prayed as she wondered what would happen when her promised husband returned.

Chapter Three

Gabe was standing in the living quarters that connected to the old trading post. No one had lived here for a long time until he moved down from the mountains this past summer. When his mother was alive, the four of them—his mother, father, Adam and him—had lived here happily enough. But since then it had no good memories for him. The floor was packed dirt. The walls were squares of thick-cut sod, piled on top of each other and melded together over time with muslin covering them so that the interior of the room was the color of bleached bones left out in the sun. One wood door led to the outside and the other led to the storeroom. Old peeled logs rose vertical around the doors and in the corners, supporting a sloped roof.

"It's not much," he admitted. The room seemed to have shrunk since he left it this morning. "I've thought about building a new place. Get some lumber down from Fort Benton."

He'd add more windows, too, he promised himself. And put in a solid floor.

The woman stood beside him silently. Her eyes were so dark, he wondered if she was in shock. Her face was pale, too. The only color on her was her chestnut hair, which was still tumbling down around her thin face. He found he liked it that way.

"Do you feel the need to sit down?" he asked cautiously.

He wasn't sure why her approval mattered to him, but he hoped she would see that this place had once been a home even if it had been years ago when his mother was alive.

"I'm not faint," she answered back, her voice weak.

He'd been afraid she'd take offense at his suggestion. She looked like she was only standing upright through sheer determination, though.

He should have waited to bring her back here until he had the lantern lit. He generally would hang it on a hook by the inside door and the light made everything a warmer yellow. His mother used to say her favorite time of the day was when everyone was safe inside and the lantern was hung for the night.

He realized he still had the pair of thick socks in his hands and held them out to Annabelle. "Here. These are for you."

The children had been asleep in front of the fire when he finished taking care of the horses and went to get the socks. Without thinking about it, he had suggested Annabelle come back here with him so they could talk without disturbing the little ones.

"Of course, this is not Adam's home," she finally said, the sense of relief evident in her voice.

"No, but he's welcome to stay anytime." Gabe wanted her to know they did have a place when she found out his brother had none. "Even when I build my new house in the spring. I'll make it big enough for everyone."

She looked at him then with confusion on her face, but didn't say anything more.

She stepped closer and took the socks. "Thanks."

The storm outside had darkened the sky so that even Gabe thought it seemed later than it was. The small glass windows at each end of this side room showed black in the gaps left by the threadbare curtains. Gabe looked around some more. A few upright boards and another thin curtain marked off the back area where the beds were. Daniel and Eliza slept in the large bed his father had brought with him decades ago when he brought his new bride back from the East Coast. Gabe replaced the feathers in the mattress each year and it was comfortable. He had never slept in that bed, making do with the small rope bed against the far wall instead. Once Adam had joined them, Gabe made a bed for himself in the pile of buffalo hides in the storeroom so that his brother could sleep near his children.

"I just put new muslin on the underside of the roof," he said, wishing he'd already started work on his new house. "You shouldn't have any dirt falling down. And the place is sturdy. The sod keeps the heat in on cold winter nights like this, too."

"I'm sure everything is very—" The woman paused. "Adequate."

Gabe winced. Knowing she was coming, he should have spent more effort and made the place look like a home. But she hadn't quite seemed real to him until she stepped off that train. Years ago, the room had looked better. Any influence from his mother had faded completely. There used to be a white crocheted doily on the back of the walnut rocking chair. Now, the chair sat unadorned near the bales of beaver pelts that were tied up in one corner by the window. He had a rope running from one of the spokes in the back of the rocker to the windowsill. He used that to stretch leather.

"I ordered this in from St. Louis." He turned and gestured to the cookstove. Neither he nor his father could make good biscuits and he had thought the stove might help. The handles on the warming oven could use some polish, but the cast iron was still a deep black. A kettle sat on the back with beans enough for supper. He'd planned to make up some corn bread to go with them, but it was getting late.

"My cousin had a stove like that," Annabelle said and he thought he detected relief in her voice. "It heats evenly. I should be able to make us a fine Christmas dinner."

"The children will appreciate that," Gabe said as the knot in his stomach relaxed. "They're tired of my cooking."

"But surely their father cooks, too," Annabelle said as she continued looking around.

A glass-globed kerosene lamp sat in the middle of the rough-hewn table. Gabe told himself that, once he lit the lamp, it would give off a soft yellow glow just like the lantern did. He was in no hurry, though. Now that she was talking, it felt strangely intimate to be here with her in the dim light.

Even with all of the shadows, Gabe could not help but notice the look on the woman's face when she mentioned his brother. She looked hopeful, but vulnerable.

"Adam can do a little of everything," he said, unwilling to let her know his brother refused to even attempt to make biscuits. He had notions that a man shouldn't do the work a woman usually did.

Annabelle turned to Gabe and smiled shyly. "He sounds very accomplished."

Gabe didn't know how to answer that, but then he heard a rustling in the doorway and figured he didn't have to say anything.

"My pa is the best at everything," Daniel said as he stood there, Gabe's jacket hanging open from his shoulders.

"He told me how he liked to surprise you and your sister with pancakes for breakfast," Annabelle said as she walked over and knelt down by the boy. "I could almost see all of you from his description."

"On pancake mornings he used to bring in lots of wood." Daniel smiled. His hair was matted and he looked tired. "He said the fire had to be hot so my ma could fry them just right."

Annabelle reached up and smoothed back the boy's hair, but Gabe noticed she frowned slightly in thought as she did so. He didn't want her to realize Adam had never cooked anything himself.

"Before we worry about breakfast, we better eat something now or we'll be starving by morning," Gabe said cheerfully as he walked over to the stove and lifted the lid on the kettle of beans. He'd put an onion and some bacon in the pot before they had left to go into Miles City. He might add a touch of molasses, too, now that they had some.

He glanced over at Annabelle and Daniel. Something had happened. The boy looked stricken. Gabe wondered what had gone wrong as he turned to them. The woman's back was stiff as she knelt there and then she started to rise. Gabe wondered if she was still thinking about Adam's cooking.

"I'll go out and get the supplies," Gabe said, not really intending to leave yet, but needing to say something. He felt a prickling at the back of his neck.

Annabelle slowly turned around. She had red spots on her cheeks and she was holding the letters Daniel had taken with them this morning. He must have stuffed them into the inside pockets of Gabe's jacket.

"This is your jacket?" she asked.

Gabe nodded.

"You have my letters, then," Annabelle said, her voice indignant. Her eyes flashed at him, her accusations apparent. "They were supposed to be private. Between me and Adam."

"I—ah…" Gabe shifted his feet. He looked down at Daniel and saw the pleading look in his nephew's eyes.

"Did you steal them after Adam left?" Annabelle demanded of Gabe then. "Is that it? I hope you enjoyed reading them. Were they amusing?"

"I didn't read them," Gabe said. He could give her that much reassurance.

Annabelle looked at him like she didn't believe him.

"The letters between a woman and a man should be private," she said. "I opened up my heart to your brother."

"Uncle Gabe always tells the truth," Daniel spoke then, his chin going out in that obstinate angle he took when he was making a stand and not counting the cost. The boy looked over at his uncle and Gabe shook his head slightly. There was no need for Daniel to earn the woman's displeasure by confessing that he was the one who had taken the letters off the shelf where his father kept them.

Annabelle turned and knelt down in front of the boy again. She looked at Daniel so tenderly that Gabe could almost see his mother doing the same to Adam all those years ago.

"You don't need to defend your uncle," she said softly. Her skirt spread around her on the dirt floor and she seemed more concerned about Daniel than the dust and wrinkles in her silk dress.

"But—" Daniel started to protest.

"Listen to Miss Hester." Gabe started to walk to the door. "I need to go out and bring in the supplies anyway. Then we'll eat."

He didn't want anyone to see the tears forming in his eyes. The cold air steadied him as he stepped outside. He didn't care if Annabelle was upset with him as long as she kept loving Daniel and Eliza the way she was doing.

It wasn't until later that Annabelle felt the anger slip away from her. Gabe had brought in enough pieces of wood to heat the living quarters for the night and she was sitting on the edge of the bed in the sleeping area, brushing her hair. They'd eaten their dinner some time ago. Daniel was asleep on the rope bed against the wall and Eliza was curled up on the bed she was going to share with Annabelle tonight.

Long shadows formed on the wall as she raised her arm with each brushstroke. She normally didn't brush her hair until she'd changed into her nightclothes, but everything today had been unusual. She had shaken out her black dress to wear tomorrow, but she still had her gray silk on. The only light was coming from the lamp on the table by the cookstove, but she must be getting used to the room as it seemed rather cozy to her now. Maybe it was the even breathing of the children as they slept or the sounds of Gabe walking around in the other part of the room.

Annabelle's letters were neatly stacked on the nearby low shelf and she looked over at them with some regret. Before he went to bed, Daniel had confessed to her that he had been the one to take her letters off that shelf and bring them to the depot. He'd added rather sheepishly that he couldn't read yet, but his father had read the one she'd written to him and Eliza aloud to them several times. The boy had looked so miserable that she had no choice but to forgive him with a hug and assure him everything was fine.

Gabe must have opened the firebox again on the stove, because a flash of light shone through the curtain that separated the bedroom from the rest of his small home.

"Would you like me to heat you some warm milk before I bed down in the store?" he asked as Annabelle heard him adjust the lids on the stove.

Annabelle leaned over so she could see around the curtain. "Yes, please. That would be nice."

She almost blushed as she looked out into the dim light. He'd just come in from checking on the horses and his hair was damp from the snow so that strands were hanging down on his forehead, reminding her of the boy he'd once been.

"I usually make some for the children," he said as he saw her. "But they're so tired tonight that it's best that they just sleep."

"I agree." She stood up and straightened the seams in her gray dress. She then patted her hair until it was tidy. He still hadn't given her the hairpins, but she wasn't going to ask about them tonight. Instead, she picked up the stack of her letters.

She walked around the curtain and into the kitchen area. Gabe was pouring two cups of warm milk and she could smell the slight sweetness of the drink.

"You're fortunate to have a cow," she said as she stepped closer to the table.

"I bought her when the children came."

She nodded, unsurprised that he would do that for them, and then set her letters on the table before pulling out one of the chairs.

"I owe you an apology," she said as she sat down. "Daniel told me he was the one who took my letters."

"He was only worried you wouldn't stay." Gabe set the cup of warm milk in front of her. "He didn't mean to do anything with them, except maybe show them to you. I'm sure he'd forgotten he even put the letters in my coat pocket."

Annabelle nodded. "He said he couldn't read them anyway."

"He needs to go to school and learn," Gabe said as he sat down, as well, and set his cup on the table. "I guess we just keep waiting for everything to become more settled before we send him."

Annabelle took a long sip of the warm milk. "You mean for Adam to become more settled, don't you?"

Gabe was silent for so long that she thought he might not answer.

Finally, he said, "Adam is a good man. If you can be patient with him, he'll be a fine husband."

Annabelle put her hand on the stack of letters almost without realizing it. "I wrote him six letters. It wasn't much, but I think he should know me from them."

The wooden planks of the table had been worn smooth with years of use. She moved her hand away from the letters and laid it by her cup. Then she looked up at the man sitting across from her.

"Adam thinks you are a wonderful woman." Gabe smiled. "You should have heard how proud he was when you agreed to marry him."

Annabelle felt suddenly very tired. "It was the hat, wasn't it? He wrote how much he liked the hat in my picture."

She wondered if she should have worn something else in her photo. That hat made her look like someone who she wasn't. It might work to attract a husband, but she was beginning to wonder if it would make it more difficult to have a congenial marriage. The only other hat she had was a small black one she'd worn to her father's funeral.

"I'm sure my brother was proud of you for more than what you wore on your head," Gabe said softly, almost as though he knew what she was thinking. "He said you would be an excellent mother."

"I love the children already." She smiled at him. He couldn't have said anything that would have soothed her heart better. She might not find love with Adam, but the children would be enough. They already accepted her. "I can't force anyone to marry me, though. I thought Adam was willing to do so, but…" Her voice trailed off.

"He'll marry you," Gabe insisted and then paused. "He just has a hard time saying goodbye. He may have told you that our father sent him east to live with our grandparents when he was four years old."

Annabelle nodded as the cup of milk grew cold in front of her.

"Adam resented it bitterly," Gabe continued. "He's having a hard time letting go of his feelings for his late wife. But he will. He just needs to wear himself out first. My grandmother said he was that way when he went back with them. He didn't settle in for months."

It took Annabelle a few moments, but she finally saw the pain hiding in Gabe's eyes.

"And how long did it take you?" she asked softly. "Before you were at peace with his leaving?"

Gabe looked surprised. "I wasn't worried about me. I wasn't the one who had been sent away. I was fine."

Annabelle nodded, but she didn't believe him. Not really. Maybe that's why she reached her hand across the table and lightly touched his. "It's all right if you were sad, too."

He looked down at the table, but not before he'd turned his hand enough to clasp hers.

The surge of warmth that she felt race up her face didn't have a trace of sorrow in it. If Adam had the same depth of feeling that his brother had, Annabelle was beginning to think he might be worth waiting for. She felt closer to Gabe than she had since she met him and she wanted him to know her better, too.

When Gabe let go of her hand, she reached over

and pulled the stack of letters to her. Then she started looking at the envelopes, one by one.

"I would like you to read one of the letters I wrote," she said as she kept sorting through the paper. She never knew how to tell people about her injuries from the fire and she had done a good job of it in the letter she'd sent to Adam.

She went all through the letters and didn't see the one she wanted.

"Is this all of them?" she asked Gabe, looking up at him.

"Adam kept your letters on that shelf. I'm sure they're all there."

"But they're not."

"If the letter came, Adam would have put it with the others. He had no other place to keep it."

They were both silent as she looked through the letters once again, this time checking to be sure two letters hadn't been put into one envelope. "I still can't find it."

She looked at Gabe. "You don't suppose it fell out of your pocket when Daniel was walking around?"

"We would have seen it." Gabe shook his head. "And I've never known the boy to be careless. Knowing him, those letters were tucked deep into that inside pocket of my jacket."

"He showed me that pocket," she said. A letter would not have blown out of it.

Gabe thought a bit longer. "I've heard people in town complain that we don't always get every piece of our mail out here in the territories. It's better since the railroad came, but sometimes a letter just never arrives."

Annabelle's heart sank. That meant Adam didn't know about her injuries. She'd been so careful to be detailed about what she could and couldn't do and he'd never read the letter. She felt foolish now for thinking that his lack of comment about her injuries had been because he was sensitive to her feelings. He might not want her for a wife even if he came back. Worse yet, he might think she was trying to trick him by not telling him about her limitations.

"The letter was important, wasn't it?" Gabe finally said.

She nodded, trying not to let her worry show. She looked up and saw Gabe watching her.

"You'll just have to tell him about it when he gets here," he said kindly as he reached over and squeezed her hand lightly. "I'm sure everything will work out fine."

Annabelle didn't know what to say so she just nodded. Gabe must know his brother better than she did. She looked at the man sitting across the table from her. His face didn't seem as forbidding as it had when she first saw it this afternoon. His forehead still creased in a slight frown and she supposed that a person glancing at his visage would think he was scowling. But she focused on his eyes now and she saw the depth of compassion in them.

"You'll have to come visit us," she said then. "When Adam and I move up to his ranch."

She saw the shift in his face. The frown deepened and he looked down at the table.

"We'll have to see what comes," he finally said.

He sounded like he didn't believe the visit would ever happen. But she nodded politely and tried not to let her disappointment show.

Before long, Gabe took a final drink from his cup and announced that he was retiring for the night.

He laid the key on the table. "Lock the door behind me."

Then he went into the storeroom. Annabelle sat at the table by herself for a few more minutes, her fingers wrapped around the cup as it grew colder.

The circle of light from the lamp seemed to spread as the night deepened.

Father. She prayed the one word and stopped. She never was certain God cared when she called Him by that name. So she cleared her throat and began again, *Lord, be with me tonight. Show me what to do tomorrow. I need your help and guidance. Amen.*

Then she went over to the door and locked it like Gabe had asked. She was just going to need to trust God that Adam would accept her.

Chapter Four

Early the next morning, Gabe stood in the lean-to and slowly put a blanket on the back of his horse. The air was icy cold and he figured a few preparations now would make his journey easier later in the day. He was in no hurry. A thin layer of snow covered the ground, but his horse was accustomed to winter weather. The only reason Gabe paused so often in grooming the animal was because he wanted to give Annabelle time to wake up before he knocked at the door to the kitchen.

He'd already milked the cow and set the bucket where the cream would rise. The few chickens he had weren't laying eggs right now, but he'd scattered a handful of field corn under their roost anyway. The children had turned him into a farmer.

But today, he had other work to do. He needed to assure Annabelle that he was going to find his brother and bring him home, if he had to tie him on the back of his horse to do it. After the way Gabe had felt, sitting at the table last night and drinking his cup of milk, he figured he should get his brother back here as fast as he could—and not just to satisfy nosy Mrs. Baker and her sister.

The truth was, he felt all too inclined to put his arms around Annabelle. He wasn't as acquainted with God as he should be, but he knew a man was forbidden to covet what belonged to his brother. That's why he'd prayed for strength to do the right thing last night. And, while some of his wanting to hold Annabelle was because he felt responsible for being the one to bring her the bad news about his brother's absence, he knew that comforting her was not all there was to his feelings.

So he was determined to wipe away any feelings for Annabelle. She was promised to his brother, and, as near as he could tell, she still wanted to marry him. Besides, there were the children to consider. They wanted her for a mother and, it seemed, she melted at the sight of them.

"So that's the way it's got to be," he muttered to himself as he ran his hands along the smooth neck of his mare. She turned to look at him with something like sympathy in her eyes and he patted her for it.

He knew it wasn't always easy to live the right kind of life. But sitting in church these past Sundays had made him want to try.

He hadn't been able to sleep last night so he sat up working on a tiny leather bag with a floral design on it. He hadn't fashioned flowers on leather before and it required concentration. It didn't stop him from wondering where his brother could have gone, though. Finally, in the middle of making a rosebud, he realized Adam wasn't the kind of man to be content with green coffee and beans for long. That meant, when he'd left the mercantile in Miles City, there was only one place he would have been headed—Fort Keogh.

Gabe was so excited when he realized where Adam was that he was halfway to the other part of the building before he stopped himself. The door was locked and he didn't want to disturb anyone's sleep. He went back to his workbench.

In the past, Adam had always found something to do at the fort that would be rewarded with an invitation to have dinner with the troops. He liked it there. In the evening, there would be a game of poker. And maybe a jug would be passed around cautiously, while a soldier kept watch for any officer who might be walking by. Since Adam didn't have money to drink and play poker in any saloon from here to Helena, the fort was the only place he would find a comfortable place to hide out.

Thinking of it now, Gabe pressed his lips together grimly. If he knew his brother, he'd regaled the troops with the story of how he'd run away from the parson's noose. Adam was popular for his humorous stories. Gabe hoped he had enough sense not to mention Annabelle. Because if Adam did say anything, all of the soldiers in the fort would find some excuse to stop by the post here. And, no matter what reason they gave for coming, Gabe would know what really brought them. They would be hoping to marry the mail-order bride themselves. Women were scarce enough around here that Annabelle would have no trouble finding another husband if his brother didn't follow through on their agreement.

Gabe felt his stomach tighten at the thought. His brother needed to get back here soon.

Gabe looked outside again to see if the sun had risen sufficiently to have awakened Annabelle. He was anxious to get over to the fort. But before he left, he needed to tell her not to let any stray soldiers into the post while he was gone. And, of course, the two of them needed to decide about the party they were having on Christmas Eve.

"I suppose Mrs. Baker will have the judge with her when she comes," he told the mare. "He'll probably want to get married, too, if he's a bachelor."

That earned him a snort.

Gabe decided that rather than standing here and fretting about things with his horse, he should go knock at the kitchen door and see if Annabelle was as worried as he was about the man she should marry and this party he'd offered to host.

Meanwhile, Annabelle had found a small mirror behind the washbasin across from the cookstove. She had taken it back to her bed and perched it on the shelf, the one that still held her letters, and then she tried to bring some order to her brushed light brown hair. She had already slipped on the black cotton dress she'd laid out last night. It was wrinkled, but it would be fine. It was her hair that was causing her to frown into the mirror. She was afraid she was going to have to braid it and leave it that way for the day.

After searching through her valise, she had gathered together five hairpins. She used to be able to put her hair in an elaborate coil with that many pins and have it perfectly secured. But, with her scars, her one elbow didn't bend as well as it used to, and she couldn't get her hair to cooperate as well as it had in the past. She needed more pins now or her hair would tumble here and there.

Not that she was going to ask Gabe for the French pins he had purchased. She hoped he would have sense enough to take them back to the clerk at the store and demand that his money be returned. She knew stores did that sometimes and, clearly, the clerk would have seen yesterday that things were unusual while they were there. The man had been so nice about the broken pear ornament; she thought he might show them some mercy over the ridiculously priced pins.

Her father would not have done so, of course, with a customer of his, but she hoped things might be different here.

She looked into the mirror again. She'd make do with a braid if she had to, she told herself, congratulating herself on being sensible, until she realized something.

"I can't wear the hat," she whispered aloud. "Not with my hair in a braid."

She sat on the bed then, glancing at the small stack of letters. Adam wouldn't even recognize her without the rose hat. Granted, it needed to be reshaped after the winds yesterday, but she had counted on fixing it up so it would look adequate.

Now she looked around in discouragement.

At least the children weren't able to see her distress. Eliza was still curled up sleeping on the other side of the bed and, a few minutes ago, Daniel had put on those huge boots he wore and slid his arms into his uncle's jacket. He looked like a walking snowman when he announced he was going to get water so she could make them all some breakfast.

Just then there was a knock at the door leading into the room from the trading post.

"Come in," she called, rushing to finish the braid she'd barely started. She had unlocked the room after she'd dressed so she, at least, didn't have to go to the door. Now her fingers flew as she crossed and re-crossed her hair. She wasn't as steady as she should be, but she figured Gabe had already seen her looking bedraggled. He might not even notice the unstylish braid. It was just a single one straight down her back like a schoolgirl would wear.

She had stepped out from behind the curtain by the time Gabe slowly opened the door and walked into the room.

"Good morning," he said softly. And then he smiled at her. "You look nice today."

She had to stop herself from bristling, but she did examine him closely. "It's still kind of dark in here."

He looked even better this morning than he had yesterday. His black beard was a little damp, probably from the snow that was still slowly falling. But his eyes were alert and his hair tidy. His shirt wasn't even wrinkled and her dress still had folds from being in her valise.

"You're welcome to light the lamp anytime you need," he said as he made his way over to the table. "I have plenty of oil for it."

Then he looked at her with so much approval in his eyes that she was uncomfortable.

"No need to waste it," she said, stepping into the room farther. Maybe he hadn't noticed her braid and rumpled dress yet. "But thanks for the compliment."

She watched him closely, but he didn't seem like he wanted to take back his words, even though there was enough light where she stood that he could see her clearly. Her father would have criticized her on the braid and the wrinkles and the scowl on her face.

"I see you're ready for work," Gabe said and she figured that was why he hadn't said anything about how she looked.

"I do have plenty to do," she agreed, more relaxed now that she understood. A scrub maid never wore her good clothes; he knew that. "If you show me where things are, I can fix us all some breakfast and we can talk about what you want me to do to get ready for the Christmas party."

That caused a cloud to cross his face.

"I wish I hadn't invited Mrs. Baker and her sister out for Christmas Eve," he said.

"You didn't have much choice." After he mentioned Mrs. Baker's thoughts on the children being adopted, Annabelle knew Gabe had done the right thing. "You can't risk them taking the children. And certainly not at Christmas."

"No," he agreed. "And I don't suppose they will expect much in the way of a party anyway."

"Oh, Mrs. Baker will expect to see that pear hanging on a Christmas tree," Annabelle disagreed as she went over to the stove. "And she'll want to see that the children are happy."

"All she cares about is whether or not Eliza has a doll," Gabe said quietly. "One with hair and silk dresses and fine-knit stockings."

Annabelle glanced over to the curtain to see if the little girl was stirring. "I do have small presents for both of the children. We can give those to them when Mrs. Baker is here. Not all children even get presents at Christmas."

Gabe sat down at the table.

"I made them each something, too," he mumbled. "But they're not store-bought."

"Presents don't need to cost money," she assured him as she sat down at the table next to him. "I'm sure the children will be very pleased."

Her father had never given her a gift and he wouldn't have considered spending his time making something for her. The only time anyone ever gave her something was when her mother gave her the gold locket from her wedding. There was a photograph of Annabelle's father on one side and a small gold coin pressed into the space where another photograph would normally go. She always thought her mother had put the coin there without telling her father—that maybe she knew Annabelle would need it someday.

She had never given much thought to the presents that parents might give their children...until now.

"What did you make?" she whispered softly as she looked back at Gabe. "I embroidered some new hand-kerchiefs. It's not much, but I put their names on them. Children like that."

"That sounds very nice," he said as he beamed at her. Then he moved his chair closer to hers and whispered, also. "I made a pair of moccasins for Daniel and a leather doll for Eliza. I don't have any clothes for the doll yet, but I plan to cut out a small blanket for her to use with it."

"I have some scraps of fabric that I brought with me. I could make a dress for the doll."

"You could?" Gabe said as he moved his chair closer yet. "Even a simple dress would be enough."

Annabelle knew he didn't realize their knees were touching. But she did; her cheeks were pink because of it. Every time they sat down at this table, they seemed to be touching each other. She wasn't sure it was entirely proper, although maybe such things were less important out here than back East. He was hopefully going to be her brother-in-law anyway.

"I have some nice silk material," she answered as she inched her chair away from him.

"Perfect."

Gabe didn't seem to notice that she'd moved.

They were both silent for a moment and then Gabe started looking around and frowning at the room like it bothered him. "I don't really want to have them back here for the party. It might not be much, but it's home."

Annabelle nodded. "I thought we'd need to have everyone sit in the store area anyway. There's more room there and that big fireplace can be cheerful. We can set the tree up beside it."

"Which means we'll need to get a tree before I go to the fort," he said as he stood up. "I better get the stove ready to make breakfast."

Gabe went over to the stove and Annabelle slipped back behind the curtain. Her valise was sitting on the floor at the end of the bed and she bent down to open it. She looked up to see if Eliza was still sleeping, but the little girl lay too still for that.

"I wonder when Eliza is going to wake up," Annabelle said with an exaggerated sigh and was rewarded with the sound of soft giggles as the girl opened her eyes.

"Almost time for breakfast," Annabelle said. "I'm going to show your uncle Gabe something and then I'll be back to brush your hair."

She was suddenly grateful that her injuries would not affect her ability to do a good job with the girl's hair. At least Eliza wouldn't have to settle for braids.

While Eliza yawned, Annabelle took hold of her valise and shoved it to the other side of the curtain. Then she walked around and put her hand inside the valise to draw out one of the remnants she had after making her gray silk dress. She searched around until she found some of the crocheted lace, as well.

She walked over to Gabe with the scraps of material.

"I think I could make a simple dress with these." She kept her voice low.

"But that silk is from your dress." Gabe whispered a protest when he saw what she held. "Are you sure?"

She nodded. "Eliza will like that her doll has a dress to match mine. Maybe later I can make a sash for Eliza to wear from the same material, too."

"I'll buy you more fabric," Gabe offered then. "The next time we're at the mercantile."

"I have enough."

And, it was true, she realized. The black cotton dress she was wearing might not have a quality dye to it and the tucks on the skirt didn't fall with any grace, but she felt content.

Right then Daniel burst through the door with his bucket of water.

"I saw rabbit tracks," he announced with excitement as he set his burden down by the stove. "It's cold out there."

"Stand by the fire and warm up while I cook us some breakfast," Gabe said and then he looked at Annabelle. "It looks like Eliza wants her hair done."

Annabelle turned and saw the little girl standing by the curtain with a small hairbrush in her hand.

"Curls?" the girl asked.

"We can try them for the party," Annabelle said as she walked over and knelt by Eliza. "Your hair will be beautiful in curls."

That satisfied the girl and she led the way behind the curtain so Annabelle could help her dress. By the time Eliza was ready for breakfast, Gabe had made some of the best pancakes Annabelle had ever eaten. And then he announced that he was going to hitch up the horses and they were all going to go looking for a Christmas tree.

Daniel's eyes went wide with delight and he explained to his sister what a Christmas tree was. It seemed the two had never had one before.

"And there's an angel on the highest top branch," Daniel finished telling Eliza.

"But we don't got an angel," the girl said as she glanced over at her uncle in worry.

"No, but we have our Christmas pear," he assured her. "We can put that on our tree."

She smiled as she remembered. "Pretty."

"And we can make some of our own ornaments," Annabelle told the children. "I used to cut out paper snowflakes when I was your age for the windows in my father's store at Christmas."

Eliza looked up at her in concern. "Didn't you get to have a tree, either?"

Annabelle shrugged. "My father didn't think we needed one. There was only the two of us for the holiday. We never had company."

"Oh," Eliza said and then she seemed to think about that for a moment before climbing down from her chair and going over to crawl into Annabelle's lap.

Annabelle blinked back a tear.

"We all get to have a tree this Christmas," Eliza said.

Even Gabe had to clear his throat. "I know just the place to find a tree. If we all help with dishes, we can be ready to go soon."

Both children scrambled down to the floor. Daniel went to get the basin for washing dishes and Eliza found the broom.

"I should have thought about a Christmas tree sooner," Gabe confessed to her, his voice thick with emotion. "If I hadn't done it to prove Mrs. Baker wrong, I wouldn't have even thought of it. And look how much it means to them."

Annabelle nodded. "Children always love Christmas. We need to read the story from the Bible, too, with them. We can start it tonight and finish it after the party."

"I could stand to read that for myself," Gabe said. "I never have really understood how it is possible. God coming to earth as a baby. That's amazing."

Annabelle was quiet for a moment then she asked, "Are you a man of faith?"

Gabe sat back in his chair and answered her thoughtfully. "I want to be. I keep listening to the preacher on Sunday mornings and I want to be." He didn't say anything for a bit. "And you?"

"I'm trusting God as best I can," she told him.

"So maybe Christmas will be a time for both of us to ask for more faith," Gabe said. "The preacher says all a man needs to do is ask."

With that, he stood up and walked over to the bucket of water Daniel had brought.

"The kettle on the stove is full of water for cleaning the dishes," he said. "But we'll need to add some cold into the basin, too."

Annabelle sat alone at the table for a moment. She'd never talked about her spiritual life with a man before. Not even the preacher back home. She'd mentioned her doubts to her friend, Christina, on the train coming out here. But she'd never had a man around who cared enough to worry about her fears or insecurities. Talking with Gabe just now reminded her of what a family should be like. She could only hope Adam was as caring as his brother.

Chapter Five

The sky was turning to dusk as Gabe rode home from Fort Keogh. He'd gotten a late start on his trip over to the fort because he'd wanted to put the tree they'd found into an old bucket before he left. That way Annabelle and the children would be able to decorate it where it stood by the fireplace in the trading post. They'd agreed to bring out the white buffalo robe he had and set it in front of the tree so the children could all sit on it. They'd have enough chairs for the adults. And Annabelle had some red ribbon she intended to string along the rocks that lined the fireplace. She also planned to boil a touch of cinnamon in water to cover the musty smell the trading post had when it was damp outside.

Christmas was coming.

The snow was light, but it still made the air heavy as Gabe wiped away the flakes that had fallen on his face. He was wearing his old mountain coat with its sheepskin collar, but Annabelle insisted he wear a knit scarf she'd pulled out of her valise, too. The soldiers had been amused, because it was bright blue and he felt as decorated as that old tree probably was about now. The men knew he'd never wear the scarf without a woman asking it of him, but he kept it around his neck happily enough anyway even when he was far from the fort.

What fools men were, he thought to himself as he smiled. All a woman had to do was fuss over them a little and they'd do almost anything.

Except for Adam, he thought in discouragement. Maybe there had been too many women fussing over his brother throughout the years. He knew their grandmother had doted on him. If it had been otherwise, maybe his brother would be more responsible now.

Gabe had discovered that Adam had gone to the fort, but was no longer there. He had gone out with some of the soldiers hunting rabbits to make a Christmas stew. Or so the story was told. Gabe suspected it had more to do with a barrel of whiskey, some cards and avoiding the bride he'd apparently heard had arrived, than any stew. But Gabe had done all he could. No one knew where the rabbits were supposed to be. So he had explained the situation to the sergeant at the fort and asked him to pass on an urgent message to his brother when he returned. The sergeant had been the one who told Gabe that his brother knew about the bride, but not the encounter with Mrs. Baker. The sergeant had looked alarmed over the fate of the children and agreed Adam needed to know what was happening on Christmas Eve. The sergeant was a reliable man so Gabe felt free to leave. Regardless of why the group of soldiers had ridden off, Gabe knew word would get to his brother without much delay if Gabe read the sergeant's concern rightly.

In the meantime, Gabe needed to go home. The party was less than two days away and he didn't want to leave Annabelle to face the preparations alone.

Especially because the guest list had grown after his path crossed that of Jake Hargrove, one of his neighbors. Jake had always been good to him so it seemed natural to invite the man, his wife and three children to come to the party and, since the man seemed so pleased with the invitation, he asked him to include the Martins, too. Eleanor Martin had been a mail-order bride and he was sure Annabelle would want to talk to her. Come to think of it, Elizabeth Hargrove had married Jake without knowing him well, either.

Maybe there was something to be said for a person marrying someone they didn't know well, he thought to himself philosophically. It sure looked like the Hargroves and Martins were as happy as any married couples had a right to be.

He guided his horse along the turn that led to the path home.

That would add seven more people to their party, and he wanted to let Annabelle know before she made that apple and raisin cake she had been talking about earlier. Jake had assured him that Eleanor would bring some of her famous Christmas tea and that his wife would make a batch of the sugar cookies his children loved to eat at the holiday. He said he'd been learning to play the fiddle and would bring that along, as well, so they could have some music.

Gabe had been so moved by his neighbor's generosity that he had poured out the story of his missing brother and the threat posed by Mrs. Baker and her sister. Jake promised to do everything he could to see that Gabe's family stayed safe and together.

They finally parted company, but not before the other man insisted on praying with him. They'd both been on horseback, but they reined their animals as close together as they could and bowed their heads. Gabe had seldom said a more heartfelt amen than he did to that prayer.

When he made the final turn that led to the old trading post, he concluded that he'd prayed with more people today, for more reasons, than he had in his entire life. And he'd found it comforting. Even if Mrs. Baker gave up her talk of adoption, he would still go to church on Sunday mornings.

The snow kept falling, but he could make out the thin trail of smoke from the cookstove. The curtains were open on the windows, but no lamp or outdoor lantern was lit. He supposed Annabelle and the children had become so intent on their paper ornaments for the tree that they had not noticed how dark it was becoming.

He didn't need to guide his horse to the lean-to. The mare knew where he was going. She quietly went into the structure and he dismounted, taking her saddle off and giving her a measure of grain before rubbing her dry.

He was at the door to the trading post before he heard the soft sobs.

He thought it was Eliza, upset about being told to go to bed. But, when he pushed the door open, he saw it was Annabelle sitting on the floor with her head down and her shoulders heaving.

"What's wrong?" he asked as he entered the room and went to her. She had lit the fire he'd laid earlier in the fireplace or he wouldn't have been able to see. The door was open to the living quarters and there was no light in there so he assumed the children were in bed.

Annabelle struggled to control her sobs and then it was silent.

It wasn't until then that he saw the Christmas tree lying on the dirt floor near her, the white paper ornaments scattered around it. Shiny bits of gold shone on the dirt, too.

Annabelle looked so defenseless sitting on the floor with her head hanging down that he reached for her as he knelt beside her. He'd intended to put his arm around her, but when his hand touched her shoulder in passing she flinched and gasped.

"You're hurt?" He didn't try to touch her again, but sat down beside her instead. "What happened?"

She lifted her tearstained face to him. "I broke the pear ornament. I wanted to move the Christmas tree. Remember how the clerk put the pear in the light so it would shine. I thought I could get the firelight to shine through it if I moved it to the right."

"But did you fall?" he asked. "I could have moved the tree for you when I got back."

She just shook her head.

Then she took a ragged breath and looked at him with distress in her eyes. "How am I going to be a good wife to Adam if I can't do something as simple as move that tree? I thought I could do it. I did not have to bend down and pick it up. I just needed to slide it over a little."

"You must have slipped. That's all," he said as he tried to figure out what had happened. "We put some water in that bucket and maybe some of it spilled."

She shook her head. "No, it's me. It's my injury—from the fire."

She looked at him fully then, strands of her chestnut hair loosened from the braid going down her back. Her green eyes were dark with misery. In the firelight, her face was pale as a piece of white china his mother had once.

"Start at the beginning and tell me all about it," he urged her.

And so she did, the words about her father's store

tumbling out of her and then she spoke of the night of the fire.

"I tried to go back in," she said, her breath catching. "My father was still in there and I needed to find him. But I couldn't. I'd stayed up late to do the bookkeeping and my father had gone to bed. The fire started on the second floor and it started burning down into the main part of the store. A piece of wood hit me across the shoulders. It was burning. I felt arms grab me from behind and start to pull me out. I didn't fight them because I thought it was my father, coming in to save me. But it wasn't him. It was Mr. Norton, our neighbor. His dog had woken him up."

She was silent for a few minutes after that and he doubted she was even aware that she had taken his hand in a death grip.

"I have scars along my back and shoulders," she finally continued. "I told Adam about them in that letter he never received. I told all the other men who had written to me, too. The way the burns healed on my arm makes it difficult for me to lift heavy things. I don't have the strength a normal woman does."

"But you're alive," he whispered. "You could have died."

"I wished I had," she said softly. "At first there was so much pain from the burns and I'd let my father die. I heard his voice calling for me and I couldn't find him. I didn't think I deserved to live after that."

Gabe opened his arms and she slid closer to him, carefully resting against his chest.

"You couldn't have saved him," he murmured into her hair as he stroked the back of her neck. "He would have understood."

She gave a bitter chuckle and looked up at him. "You didn't know my father. He expected me to come all right."

Gabe had a fair idea of what the man was like. "Well, any reasonable parent would have understood. There are just some things you can't do."

They were quiet for a while, just sitting together in the light from the fire.

"Do you think your brother ever understood?" she finally asked. "When you didn't convince your father to let him stay with you here?"

He owed her the truth after what she'd told him. "I still hear his sobs sometimes in my dreams. I wish I had known what to say to make my father change his mind. No, I'm not sure he ever will forgive me."

She nodded then, like that was the answer she'd expected.

"Adam might not understand why he didn't get that letter then, either," she said calmly. "He might think I didn't send it. That I am trying to trick him."

"Trick him?" Gabe reared back in amazement. "Why, Adam is fortunate you agreed to marry him. A few scars don't have anything to do with that. His problem isn't with you. It's all with himself."

"None of the other men kept writing to me after that letter," she said.

"Well, they were fools," Gabe said. "Why, you were

very brave for even trying to reach your father. That's more important than whether or not you can lift something."

Annabelle looked at him then with hope in her eyes. "Do you really think so?"

"Absolutely."

He sat there enjoying the expression on her face for a moment and remembered. "Adam will think so, too. You'll see."

He wondered if the light in her eyes didn't dim just a little. Then he heard a slight sound at the doorway to the kitchen and turned to see Daniel standing there in his nightclothes.

"Eliza is scared," he informed them.

The boy sounded a little worried himself.

"Everything's fine," Gabe said as he stood up and held out a hand to assist Annabelle. "We just had a bit of an accident."

"The tree will be fine," Annabelle assured him, too.

Gabe smiled. He knew Daniel well enough to know it wasn't the tree that the boy was fretting over. His eyes hadn't left Annabelle long enough to even notice anything else.

"I'll make us all a cup of warm milk," he said as he gently encircled Annabelle's waist. He wanted to be sure she didn't fall again as they walked to the kitchen. "Then maybe we'll read a bit of the Christmas story."

Daniel's eyes lit up at that. "Will we get to the part about the angel? Eliza says she wants to see an angel for Christmas."

"Does she now?" Gabe said as they walked through the door into the kitchen.

He figured he'd already seen his angel in the faces of his niece and nephew and now there was Annabelle. A man's heart could only take in so much and his was full, if only for tonight. He hoped his brother came home by Christmas Eve, but for this evening Gabe intended to drink his fill of Christmas warmth. He knew he couldn't say the words to tell any of them how important they had become to him. But he would work tonight on their gifts, especially Annabelle's. And then he realized there was something else he could do to boost her spirits. He could use his leather tools to reshape that rose-colored hat she was so fond of.

Annabelle woke up early the next morning and lay in bed to savor the day. The warm milk had relaxed her and the words of the angel's visit to the shepherds had comforted her just like they had others like her for generations. She doubted Mary had been prepared for company on Christmas Eve any more than she and Gabe were. And yet all had been well. Of course, she reminded herself, Mrs. Baker hadn't been one of the shepherds. And, knowing men, none of them had searched out any forgotten dust in the corners of the manger.

Annabelle stared at the muslin ceiling as she thought about what she had to do today. She had cleaned her silk dress as best as she could, but she was saving that for the party tomorrow. Her black mourning dress was already dirty after all of her cleaning yesterday so she'd put it on again when she got out of bed. She'd wear her hair in the braid while she worked, but she had an idea for how to put her hair up with her five pins and she'd try that for the party.

As she sat up, she realized she had thought she'd feel worried after telling Gabe about her injuries, but she hadn't felt so lighthearted for months. Maybe the men out West weren't as worried about things like that as she had imagined.

The sun rose enough for light to come into the small window at the front of the living quarters and shine through the curtain that separated the bed area. Annabelle carefully got out of the bed so she wouldn't disturb Eliza. Both children were still sleeping. She had heard Gabe go in the kitchen a few minutes ago to build a fire in the cookstove, but he had left shortly thereafter and closed the door that led to the main storeroom. Neither one of them had remembered to lock the door after reading the Bible with the children last night.

The chill of the air made Annabelle slip on her dress quickly and search for the heavy socks Gabe had given her that first night. Her fingers were stiff, but she managed to braid her hair with no trouble. She decided to put her shoes on out by the stove so she picked them up and slipped past the curtain.

"Oh." She stopped where she stood and stared at the table.

She blinked, but the vision of her hat didn't go away. There it sat, looking as good as the day she'd worn it for her photograph. After the wind and dampness the first night she'd been here, it had taken on the shape of a mushroom. And the rose flower petals had curled up until they looked more like thorns. But someone had pushed the top back into place and made the petals look the way they were meant to be.

She was almost afraid to touch it, so she went over to the door and knocked softly instead.

Gabe opened the door with such a wide grin on his face that she forgot about the hat and just stood there gawking.

"Do you like it?" he asked, bringing her back to the present.

"I don't know how you did it," she whispered. "It's like new."

He looked pleased. "I can't wait to see you wear it again."

She nodded. It wasn't totally proper to have a hat on one's head inside a home, but she might make an exception for tomorrow. She could use the confidence that hat gave her for the party tomorrow.

Gabe stepped into the kitchen then and walked over to pick up the bucket. "The fire's going so we'll heat up some water. Then I'll make us some more pancakes. You can sit and rest a bit. We'll be busy enough later."

Annabelle decided she would do just that. She wanted to feel the sides of her hat anyway. Gabe must have worked most of the night on her hat. She only hoped he wasn't disappointed. They both knew that that hat had made her look good to his brother.

If Adam did make it back in time for the party, she wanted to be as charming as she could be. The past couple of days she'd felt so comfortable with Gabe and the children that she'd forgotten it was Adam who she needed to win over. He was the one who had offered her a place in his family. And, while he might be having difficulties right now, she could only pray that he would stand by his proposal.

She closed her eyes. It might help, she thought, if she pictured the ranch Adam had written about. She used to sit like this at night in her cousin's house before she drifted off to sleep. She had a full image of what the place looked like. Of course, the ground would be covered with snow instead of green grass at this time of year, but the wide porch on the house would still be there, along with the rocking chairs he'd mentioned they would sit in to watch the sunset. She wondered suddenly if the children had a swing near the house. If they didn't, she told herself, she'd see to it that one was built for them. Children needed to play some when the work was done.

"Miss Annabelle."

She heard the whisper and opened her eyes to see Daniel standing there in his nightclothes.

"Do you feel okay?" he asked, his forehead furrowed with worry.

"I'm just fine," she told him and opened her arms.

He came to her and she hugged him to her. "We're all going to be fine."

Then she drew back a little and smoothed down his hair. "And your uncle is going to make pancakes for breakfast so you better run and get dressed for the day."

She stood up as the boy ran back behind the curtain. She'd start the day by looking into the other part of the trading post and seeing what needed to be done. The door opened soundlessly and she stepped into the dim room. There were only embers in the fireplace, but there was enough light for her to see that the Christmas tree was standing upright again, the white snowflake ornaments hanging from its limbs and the pieces of glass from the broken pear all swept up.

She shook her head, wondering again when Gabe slept.

Just then the door opened in the living quarters and she walked back. She was going to have to find some way to thank him. Words seemed inadequate for all he'd done. She had made a handkerchief for Adam as well as the children, but she hadn't known Gabe would be with them for Christmas and it was too late to make anything now, especially with all the work they needed to do for the party tomorrow.

If she had a way to go back to the mercantile in Miles City, she would buy him one of those knife sheaths with the design of an eagle on them. Someone had done beautiful work on them and a man would be proud to carry something like that with him whether he stayed down here or went back up into the mountains. Surely she had enough money left to buy one. The thought of doing something nice for him made her feel good.

Chapter Six

Gabe could smell the apple and raisin cake baking from where he stood in the trading post. It was the day of the party, and with the pine branches that Annabelle had placed around, the air smelled better in here than it had in years. He stopped scrubbing the window and leaned against the sod wall for a moment. He doubted anyone would be looking through the windows tonight, but he wanted them clean anyway.

He'd put new muslin over the ceiling an hour ago and swept the hard dirt floor. The white buffalo robe was spread out in front of the tree. Two straight-back chairs stood beside the fireplace. They'd add more chairs later. Annabelle hadn't had a chance to drape her red ribbons around yet, but she would when the cake was baked.

Right now, she had Daniel sitting at the table in the kitchen, tracing the letters in his name. She said it might be important to Mrs. Baker that they were making sure Daniel had some education. Gabe had never thought of that, but he suspected she was right.

Eliza was taking a nap. Annabelle had told her she needed to do that because of the party tonight, but Gabe knew Annabelle had used some of the girl's nap time to work on the silk dress for her doll. The dress was basted and Annabelle planned to sew the seams after she finished with Daniel.

Hoofbeats sounded and Gabe turned to look outside. He had a fire burning to heat this room and a thin layer of frost had already started to form on the window. But it was clear who was coming down the path in the open wagon—Jake and Elizabeth Hargrove. The sky was cloudless and no snow was falling. The day was warmer than the ones that had come earlier this week.

"We have company," Gabe called out as the Hargroves climbed down from their wagon. Jake always traveled with a buffalo robe over his shoulders, and Elizabeth wore a red knit scarf like the one Annabelle had made Gabe wear.

"Already?" Annabelle squeaked in alarm from the other room and he heard her rushing to the window.

"It's just the Hargroves," he assured her. "They're not here for the party yet. They know we're still getting ready."

Annabelle had mentioned several times that she would need to change to her silk dress before any of their guests arrived. And she planned to wear her hat, she said. And a black ribbon around her neck.

By now, Gabe could see that the other couple was almost to the front door of the trading post so he opened it wide. "Come in out of the cold."

Annabelle stepped into the room, wiping her hands on an apron she'd taken out of her valise earlier. As far as Gabe was concerned, she looked just fine with her black dress and white apron. She had a serenity about her that wasn't present when she was dressed in her finery. But he knew women liked to be fashionable.

Jake and Elizabeth stomped the snow off their feet in front of the door and then stepped inside. Gabe closed the door behind them.

Elizabeth rubbed her hands together. "It's good to be out of the cold."

"Come into the kitchen and I'll make some tea," Annabelle offered.

"We can't stay," Jake said. "We're headed into Miles City and need to get back in time to get dressed for your party. Elizabeth has a new dress. But I wanted to let you know that a soldier stopped by our place earlier today and asked us to pass along the message that Adam is coming back."

"It's about time," Gabe said, not feeling as happy about it as he should.

"You're going into Miles City?" Annabelle asked in delight, as if she hadn't even heard that Adam would be here soon.

When Elizabeth nodded, Annabelle asked to speak to her in the kitchen.

"Order anything you need for the party," Gabe

called after her as the two women walked through the doorway. "Just tell the clerk to put it on my account."

When the women had left the room, Gabe turned to Jake and shook his head. "Do you have a younger brother? Sometimes they can make you grit your teeth and say things you shouldn't."

Jake nodded with a slight smile. "I used to get annoyed with mine, too. But he's been dead for several years now and I miss him."

"Oh, I'm sorry. I didn't know."

"There's no reason you should know," Jake assured him. "He was my half brother. We shared a father and his mother was a full-blooded Sioux. He died in the wars with the white men. But he left me his two daughters to raise so I think of him often. The oldest one looks like him."

Gabe nodded. "I remember hearing about that now. I was up in the mountains when your nieces were starting school and everything. I heard there was quite the storm about it all. I believe Mrs. Baker was behind that one, too."

Jake shrugged. "People don't always like to accept people who are different from them. But they've come around—even Mrs. Baker. It just took time and prayer."

They were silent for a minute.

"It makes my brother look better," Gabe finally said grudgingly. "He might have left me to handle his troubles, but at least he's still here so I can argue with him about it."

Jake chuckled. "I'll admit there were many times I wanted to scold my brother for dying. His daughters missed him something fierce at first. I thought we'd never get used to each other."

Gabe nodded. He supposed that, in time, the Stone family would have all of their differences resolved, too.

The two men were quiet, their heads bowed slightly although not in prayer. Gabe could hear the murmur of the voices in the kitchen and he wondered what spice he had forgotten. Maybe Annabelle wanted ginger for something.

Just then Jake looked up abruptly. "I know what I forgot. The soldier also said to tell you to put the coffeepot on. Several of the enlisted men announced they were going to come visit you as soon as they could get some leave."

"They don't need leave to make the trip down here," Gabe said. "It doesn't take long to ride a horse between here and the fort."

"I think they want to spend some time courting once they get here," Jake said with a grin. "Your brother is going to have some competition."

"It's his own fault if he's been telling people about Annabelle coming and him not being there to meet her," Gabe said, his irritation coming out stronger than he had intended.

Jake gave him a long, measuring look. "That bothers you, does it?"

"Of course," Gabe said. "Our mother raised us to

be more polite than that. He should have at least met her. She's a wonderful woman."

Jake nodded, but didn't say any more.

The door to the kitchen opened and the two women walked back into the trading post. They still had their heads together and were talking low and easy. Then Annabelle laughed, a sound pure as a bell.

"I've never heard her laugh like that," Gabe muttered to himself and then realized Jake could hear him.

The other man smiled. "My Elizabeth can get most people to laugh."

Within minutes, the Hargroves had their scarves and gloves on and were stepping through the door again, turning back to wave when they reached their wagon.

"I wish they could have stayed," Annabelle said with a sigh. "She's a nice lady."

"They'll be back tonight," Gabe said as he stood there wondering how he was going to say what else he needed to tell Annabelle.

Finally, he decided there was no way to say it without being blunt. "Not all our company will be so nice and polite today. I've told you before. If any soldiers stop, I don't want you to let them in unless I'm here with you."

"Well, goodness," she said. "If you're not here, they won't want to stop anyway. It's you they'd be coming to see."

"No, it's you."

"Me? Well, whatever would they want with me?"

"I reckon most of them will want you to marry them," Gabe said and was rewarded by the look of astonishment on her face.

Annabelle swallowed hard. "But they don't even know me."

"Couples get acquainted fast around here. Courting can happen in an hour or two. There aren't many eligible women for a man to set his eye on."

Some of the color was coming back into Annabelle's face.

"But I'm not eligible," she said indignantly. "I'm engaged."

And Gabe figured that said it all in her mind. He suspected the army men would have another interpretation after hearing Adam say he wasn't going to be married. And they wouldn't take a polite refusal as easily as Annabelle thought.

Annabelle had one cake cooling on the table and she'd mixed up the batter for another one. She hadn't really believed Gabe when he said a soldier or two might come by to visit. But there were six in the trading post now, drinking coffee with Gabe and waiting for her to cut the cake.

She wouldn't have offered to feed them at all, but she couldn't set aside the fact that they were serving in her country's military. It seemed unfeeling not to give them even a small piece of the cake when the smell of it baking had spread throughout the trading post.

"Ma'am." A young soldier, no older than twenty,

stood in the doorway, holding his hat. His uniform was pressed. "I was wondering if I could carry something for you."

"I'll put the cake on a plate in a minute," Annabelle said. She wasn't ready to leave her sanctuary yet. She'd never sat in a circle with six men, all of whom wanted to talk to her. It sounded a little exhausting. Of course, it might cure her shyness.

When she couldn't put it off any longer, Annabelle loaded seven pieces of fresh cake onto the plate. The cake was heavy and would stay together if the men held it in their hands to eat it.

She gave the plate to the young soldier and he started carrying it toward the door into the trading post. He walked so carefully that she wished she had cut the pieces bigger. But she didn't know how many soldiers would come today and she didn't have more ingredients to make more cakes. The one in the oven would have to do for the party.

Gasps of pleasure greeted her as she stepped through the door, although she had to admit most of the soldier's eyes were on the cake and not on her. Only Gabe was looking at her and he was frowning.

"I have another cake in the oven," she assured him quietly as she walked over to him. He had his shirt-sleeves rolled up to his elbows. "We'll have plenty for tonight."

"I'm not worried about tonight."

She didn't even respond to that. Instead, she looked around. There were only three soldiers sitting in chairs around the fireplace. Not more than fifteen minutes ago there had been six of them. It seemed some of them discouraged easily.

She told herself it was for the best, but it was still a little unnerving. First six men were intent on talking to her and now there were only three. She couldn't help but wonder if those three men who left had heard something about her. Maybe she was expected to tell the men why she'd make a good wife. That would be daunting.

"I sent half of them out to cut us some wood," Gabe said then, no doubt having watched as she looked around. "We're going to need a big fire tonight and I figure three at a time talking to you will be enough."

"Well, you could have told me you did that," she said tartly.

"None of the soldiers are going to leave without a piece of that cake and a chance to talk to you. You don't have to fret."

That made her feel better.

But twenty minutes after she'd sat down to converse, Annabelle was exhausted. How many different ways could she answer the question about what she desired in a husband? She mentioned age. She didn't want to marry anyone younger than twenty-seven years old. She was thirty and that seemed reasonable. No, she didn't care how much money a man had, although she did admit she was partial to having a roof over her head and meals on the table. She didn't want to go hungry or live in a tent or a wagon.

She expected the next question to be what kind of a wife she would be, but no one asked that.

"Does he need to be tall?" one of the men asked instead. He was shorter than her, a slight, thin man with a sad expression.

She started to say that she preferred shorter men when she looked over at Gabe and realized he was about to say something.

"If you're a mean-spirited, large man, you can leave right now," he said as he glared at each of the soldiers in turn until they hunched over in their seats. Then he turned a protective eye toward her.

She smiled at him as she realized something.

"Tall or short, slender or stocky, good men come in all shapes and sizes," she said after a moment. "I used to think most large men were mean, but I know now that's not true."

The soldiers were looking at Gabe warily now, but he was sitting proud.

"A churchgoing man is important," she offered. "A man who prays and trusts God."

"I can recite the books of the Bible," the young soldier who had carried the cake in announced. "I can do them for you right now if you want."

"Maybe we could do them later," Annabelle said gently. "I don't have much time so I think we need to change places with the other soldiers. Before you go, though, I want you all to know that I was injured in a fire not long ago. I had some burns across my back, shoulders and arm."

There was a chorus of sympathetic murmurs.

She waved them away. "The burns have healed, but I can't lift things with my arms like I used to be able to do. Anyone who marries me needs to know I have limitations."

The soldiers seemed to accept her injuries better than the other men she'd told with her letters. Still, the first group of soldiers went outside to relieve their friends so they could come in and visit with Annabelle.

The questions were nearly identical and Annabelle finally realized the men had come just to talk with her. Most of them probably weren't even interested in marriage. All they wanted was a bit of home around Christmas. She probably reminded the younger ones of their mothers.

She let them stay longer than she should have and then she had to rush to prepare for the evening. She and Gabe had cleaned the trading post the best that they could. Every corner had been dusted, although he had blocked off an area where he said he worked.

She threaded some red ribbon around the rocks in the fireplace and laid fresh pine branches under the tree. Then she pronounced the house ready and went to change into her silk dress. She was able to coil her hair on top of her head with no difficulty. Slipping the pins into her hair had taken more time, but she managed. She sat her hat on top of her head as Gabe called out that Mrs. Baker's buggy was coming down the road. She hoped it wasn't too long before the Hargroves and Martins arrived. She'd prayed while she dressed, asking God to show Mrs. Baker that the children belonged with their family.

Lord, don't let her frighten them, either. Annabelle said a final prayer as she adjusted her hat.

Chapter Seven

No sooner had the soldiers left than Gabe watched Mrs. Baker step over the threshold to enter the trading post carefully, almost as though she was afraid her shoes would find something sticky on the other side. Dusk had begun to darken the sky as her brother-in-law pulled the buggy to a stop and the inside of a building was naturally dim. Maybe the older woman just couldn't see well. She was wearing a smaller hat than before, but she had a glittering brooch that was sure to catch Eliza's eye. Gabe resigned himself to the fact that his niece would likely be as fascinated with the older woman tonight as she had been in the mercantile.

"Here's a nice chair for you in front of the fire," he said as he pulled one forward a little. He was grateful that the judge had not come with Mrs. Baker. Maybe he wasn't even visiting Miles City this Christmas.

"Why, thank you." The woman seemed surprised at his gesture.

"My mother raised Adam and me to be polite," he said without thinking, his words clipped. Then he realized he should say more. "We plan to teach Daniel and Eliza the same ways."

Mrs. Baker just nodded as she sat down.

No one challenged Gabe with the fact that he was the uncle and not the father of the children.

So he turned to the older couple who had also come into the room with Mrs. Baker. "I'm afraid I never did get your full names. I'm Gabe Stone. Annabelle Hester, my brother's fiancée, will be here any minute. She's fixing my niece's hair."

"I don't suppose they're going to put her hair in ringlets?" the woman in the couple asked eagerly. "Our Mary always loved to have her hair done that way."

"I don't believe so," Gabe answered as he pulled forward another chair. If he thought there was any chance Eliza would come out here in ringlets, he would go warn Annabelle to wrap a towel around the girl's head. The less she looked like the couple's little Mary, the better it was for everyone.

"We're the Smiths," the older man said as he gestured for his wife to take the chair. "Virginia and Edgar Smith. From Maryland."

Virginia sat down in the chair and Gabe pulled out another one for her husband.

"Pleased to meet you, I'm sure," Gabe muttered and then he stood there. With everyone seated, there didn't seem to be anything more to do.

"It's a lovely tree," Mrs. Smith finally murmured.

"I know children enjoy making ornaments and those are wonderful snowflakes."

Gabe heard the door open to the kitchen.

"I see you don't have the glass pear any longer," Mrs. Baker added in what sounded like satisfaction. "The tree would have looked better with it. But I thought you might have to sell it."

Annabelle took a step into the room, looking resplendent in her rose hat and gray silk dress, with the tucks all pressed and the fabric shining softly in the glow of the fire. "I broke the glass pear."

Her voice had more than a hint of guilt.

"We found we really didn't need it," Gabe said at the same time.

Mrs. Baker nodded like she made sense out of what they'd said.

Eliza had walked in with Annabelle, her hand clutching some of the woman's dress. Daniel had followed on the other side of Annabelle, but none of their guests were watching him.

"Oh, she's such a sweet child," Mrs. Smith said with an emotion-filled glance to her husband. "And she looks so dressed up."

Annabelle had swept the girl's hair back in some twisted thing that Gabe didn't understand. And her blue dress had been washed yesterday and pressed this morning. Gabe had never seen her looking so ready for company. She rewarded the older ladies with a smile and Gabe almost grinned himself.

Just then Gabe heard the sounds of a wagon outside and he went to the door.

"It's the Hargroves," he informed the others. "And it looks like they have the Martins with them." He turned to everyone around the fireplace. "The rest of our guests for the evening. I think you'll enjoy them."

Gabe was relieved when he saw that Jake had his fiddle in his hand as he started walking toward the door. Gabe wasn't sure how long he could keep up the idle chatter with Mrs. Baker.

The Hargroves and their children spilled through the door first, seeming to fill up the room with their joyful greetings to everyone. And the Martins followed close behind them. It took a few minutes to get everyone's coat off and the cookies they'd made delivered to the kitchen. Then it didn't take much to convince Jake to play a few tunes on his fiddle. He began with "Away in the Manger" and ended with "Silent Night."

Jake missed some of the notes and made up others as he went, but his enthusiasm had them all smiling. The sun was gradually going down and Gabe lit a lantern to set on a shelf by the fireplace. In its light, the paper snowflakes on the tree almost shone. This really was a Christmas party.

When Jake couldn't play a particular carol on his fiddle, he'd sing it instead and they'd all join in. Gabe couldn't remember ever having such a wonderful evening. He was almost disappointed when Annabelle announced it was time for cake and cookies. They had already agreed that was when the party would start to end.

By the time Mrs. Baker and the Smiths were starting to put their coats back on, Gabe was almost sorry the evening was over. He knew they had to drive back into Miles City, though, and wouldn't want to do it much later in the night.

An angry pounding started at the door about then.

Gabe's heart sank as he looked over at Mrs. Baker. She had a smug look on her face and he figured she had the same suspicions about who was on the other side of the door as he did.

"Give me a minute," he said as he stepped over to answer the door. He figured that, if he could slip out and talk to his brother, maybe he could quiet him long enough for everyone else to leave. It didn't work that way. When Gabe opened the door, he put his arm on the door frame to prevent Adam from walking in. His brother was determined, though, and quickly bent down and ducked under Gabe's arm.

Once he was inside, Adam started to sway.

"What's this?" He slurred out the words. His eyes were bloodshot and he hadn't shaved in several days. "Having a party and I'm not invited?"

"You were invited," Gabe said curtly. "You were just off hunting rabbits instead. Now if you'll let me take you into the living quarters and let me show you a bed for the night, we can all get some rest."

Adam shook his head and leaned closer to Gabe. He reeked of whiskey. "I don't want to go to bed. There's a party. I like parties." He looked around the room again and his gaze stopped at Eliza. "There's my little girl. Come to Daddy."

Eliza didn't move. She almost looked frightened, with her big eyes and her bottom lip quivering slightly.

This was not what Mrs. Baker should see, Gabe told himself, as he took his brother by the arm and started to walk him into the living quarters. "Let me get you some coffee."

He glanced over at Annabelle. "I'm sure Mrs. Baker and the Smiths want to be on their way. Take the lantern to the door so they don't stumble before lighting the lantern on their buggy."

"Don't think we don't see what condition your brother is in," Mrs. Baker said firmly as she tied a scarf around her head. "My cousin, the judge, will be hearing about it. It's a disgraceful way to spend Christmas Eve."

"We'll talk about it later," Gabe said as he opened the door to go into the kitchen, guiding his brother through the opening. Gabe was all bluff, though. He didn't know what he could say to make Adam sound like a reasonable parent.

Annabelle felt her heart sink as she watched her fiancé being taken from the room. She had seen men drunk before, but it wasn't a sight she wanted to see on a regular basis.

"Let me get that lantern for you," she said to Mrs. Baker as she fought back hot tears of embarrassment.

How could Adam show up like this? Didn't he know Mrs. Baker would use everything against him that she could?

She lifted the lantern off the shelf and held it as she walked to the door. She glanced up at Mrs. Baker and was surprised to see a look of sympathy on her face.

"I truly do want what is best for the children," the older woman said then, looking at Annabelle. "I doubt your Adam has been sober for more than a day or two in the past month."

"I'm not sure he's my Adam anymore," Annabelle managed to say as she pulled the door open and stood there in the cold, without a coat or shawl. The truth was he might have never been her Adam even though he'd become her dream.

She looked down when she felt a tiny fist tug on the skirt of her dress. She put her hand on Eliza's head, feeling the coils of hair underneath her fingers. Maybe tomorrow she'd wrap the girl's hair in curling rags.

She waited for the buggy to start back into Miles City before she closed the door. When she turned around, Elizabeth Hargrove took a few steps toward her and opened her arms. Annabelle walked into them without hesitation.

"Don't you worry now," the other woman said as she patted her shoulder. "We're going to be praying for God to redeem Adam's life. And for guidance for you, too."

"I have trouble trusting Him," Annabelle admitted.

"He'll take care of you," Elizabeth said with a confidence that made Annabelle believe it, too.

All of the Hargroves and Martins wanted to pray with her before they left and she was happy for them to do so. Not long after that Gabe came to the door and said she and the children could go inside the living quarters. He and Adam were going to bunk down by the fire in the main part of the trading post for the night.

She and the children were all so tired it did not take them long to scramble into bed and fall asleep. She and Gabe had finished the presents and they had planned earlier to let the children open them after breakfast on Christmas Day. By then Adam would be sober, she thought to herself. Maybe he had some good reason for being as drunk as he was. She needed to listen to him before she made a decision about what to do. Every man deserved that courtesy. But the thought didn't give her any pleasure.

Her last thought before falling asleep was that she should write her friend, Christina, and tell her that her fiancé hadn't prompted a flutter around her heart at all. The feeling she had was more like a deadweight sitting on top of her head.

Annabelle had been asleep for hours when something woke her up. It was dark in the room, but she did see a strip of light coming from under the door leading to the main part of the trading post. Gabe must have lit the lantern again since it gave off more light than the fireplace. She wondered if he needed help with his brother. He'd made coffee earlier, but he'd left the pot in the kitchen. She heard the murmur of voices then and decided to go to the door and tell Gabe she would heat up the coffee for them if they wanted it.

She slipped her robe on and put her socks on her feet. Her hair was in the braid she usually wore it in at night. She wasn't looking the way she'd like to when her fiancé saw her for the first time when he was sober, but she figured it was so dark that it would make little difference. And, after the night he'd had, he wouldn't likely remember anyway.

The door was not locked and she opened it slightly. Gabe and Adam were standing near the fireplace, their heads bent toward each other in intense conversation.

"But she's got something wrong with her," Adam was saying. He wasn't drunk now, but his voice was still thick from it. "The men who were here earlier today said she had scars and burns and couldn't even lift much of anything. Who needs a wife like that?"

"You do," Gabe said with a hiss in his voice. She could see the barely restrained anger in him from the way he stood with his legs spread apart and his hand in a fist at his side. "Those things don't matter. Annabelle is wonderful. She has more love to give than anyone I know. And she's smart and brave and—" he paused to catch his breath "—much too good for you."

Annabelle knew she should step back and close the door. Neither brother knew she was here listening, but she couldn't seem to move.

"Well, I always did like that hat," Adam said with

a little more warmth in his voice. "She had it on to-night or I wouldn't have known her. She's a plain little thing, isn't she?"

"You must be blind," Gabe shot back. "She's beautiful. Watch her eyes. They change color slightly as she goes through different emotions."

"If you say so." Adam yawned. "I wonder if she has any money. I didn't win like I thought I would at the fort poker game. I can't start the ranch back up without some money."

"Then I suggest you get a job," Gabe said as he ran his hands through his hair. He looked tired.

Annabelle wondered if either of the men had slept any this night as she quietly closed the door again. A little light came in the window of the kitchen now so morning must be coming before long. She walked over to the table and sat down.

She didn't move for a few minutes. She kept expecting a wave of pain to wash over her. She'd just found out her Adam wasn't interested in marrying her. Oh, Gabe might be able to convince him to do so, but she just didn't see how that would be something good.

She bowed her head slightly. Elizabeth Hargrove might have firm confidence that Annabelle could trust God, but she realized she'd never had to trust Him like she was going to now. She wasn't going to marry Adam Stone and she didn't know what else she would do. She didn't have enough money to go back to her cousin. None of the soldiers that had come by had really proposed to her and, given Adam's words, it was not likely they would. She even understood. Life was hard here in the West and there was a lot of work to be done. No man needed a wife who couldn't do all that was needed.

She sat at the table until she grew chilled. Then she went back to bed and lay there. She wouldn't say anything to anyone tomorrow. It was Christmas Day. But on the day after, she would need to make plans. Maybe there was a job she could do in Miles City.

No tears came even though she kept expecting them. Maybe she was too weary to cry. The journey here had been long and she had traveled far. She was doing her best to trust God, but He wasn't leading her where she needed to be.

Forgive me my doubts, she prayed even as she felt them fill her.

Chapter Eight

Gabe had woken Adam and made sure his collar was straight before he sat him down in one of the chairs still by the fireplace.

"So, what's it going to be?" Gabe said, not bothering to cover the irritation and harshness in his voice. He hadn't slept much last night and he didn't expect to get any rest today.

"About what?" Adam replied.

"You know what! You promised your children a mother for Christmas so, if you're going to do it, you better ask her today."

Gabe had a sour feeling in his stomach, but someone needed to do something for his brother's family.

"Do you think I need to ask? That's why she came out here from the East Coast."

Gabe gave a bitter laugh. "After all you've put her through? Yes, I think you need to ask. And I'd do it nicely if I were you."

Adam took a deep breath and nodded. "I suppose you're right."

Then he started walking toward the door that led to the other part of the building.

"Now?" Gabe asked in sudden panic. "You're going to ask her now?"

Adam turned and shrugged. "Why not? I might want to go back to the fort later today. So I should get it over with."

Gabe swallowed back every protest that wanted to come out of his mouth. He gave a curt nod then and reached for his coat. "I'm going to go out and feed the horses, then."

With that, Gabe stomped over to the heavy door and went outside. The morning was cold and he welcomed the discomfort. If he had his choice, he'd be farther away from here today than just the lean-to, but the children were expecting Christmas morning and he wouldn't disappoint them. At least the proposal should make his niece and nephew happy. And Annabelle, too. He told himself his brother would settle down and be a decent husband when he actually said his marriage vows again.

He gave some oats to the horses first and then sat down to milk the cow. Being with the animals gave him some peace. Things had shifted last night between him and his brother. They had been closer than they had since Adam came home from back East almost ten years ago. Maybe all it had taken was a crisis to bring them together.

He had the pail filled when Adam came into the lean-to and threw a saddle on his horse.

"Aren't you even staying for breakfast?" he asked.

Adam laughed. "No. I've got too much to celebrate."

Then Adam got on his horse and rode away.

Gabe shook his head. He doubted Annabelle would be too happy with receiving a proposal and then having her fiancé leave like this. No woman would like that.

He picked up the pail full of milk and started back to the house. He'd have to congratulate her anyway.

Gabe set the pail in the trading post and then walked over to knock on the door to the living quarters. Annabelle's quiet voice told him to come in, and, when he opened the door, he saw her and the children sitting at the table. They all looked excited.

"We've been waiting for you," Annabelle said with a grin.

"We have presents," Eliza added, her eyes twinkling.

Gabe had forgotten about the presents. Fortunately, he and Annabelle had gathered them all together yesterday afternoon before the party. He saw that she had the bag on the floor beside her.

"I'm ready." Gabe sat down and resolved to be as excited as the children.

Annabelle passed out the presents, one by one.

Daniel got the moccasins from Gabe first and rushed to put them on his feet. "They fit!"

Eliza looked at her leather doll in wonder and touched the silk dress that the doll wore. "Pretty."

Each child got a handkerchief with their name embroidered on it from Annabelle, and Daniel traced the letters.

"Now I'll always have my name with me," he said.

Gabe shyly handed over the present he had for Annabelle. He'd finished the small leather bag that had the French hairpins inside.

"Why, it's beautiful," she said as she examined the floral design he'd made in the leather. "I had no idea there were such small bags for sale in the mercantile."

"I made it," he told her.

She looked at him in shock. "You're the one who makes those leather goods that were on display."

Her voice sounded distressed.

"Yes, but it's not a problem."

She shook her head and started to laugh. Then she held up a paper bag. "It is since this is the present I got for you."

She handed him the bag and he pulled out the knife sheath. He grinned then. "It always was one of my favorite designs."

"And I wanted to get you something to remember me by," she said, still shaking her head.

"I'll never forget you." He said the words before realizing they might not be appropriate since she was engaged to his brother—recently engaged after this morning. He squeezed out the next words. "Of course, I won't forget you. Not when you're married to my brother."

He supposed he should stand up and make pancakes. The children would be expecting that next. And, he didn't want to sit at the table and let his sadness grow. There'd be time enough for grieving when he was alone.

"I'm not marrying your brother," Annabelle said softly.

Gabe looked at her. "He was supposed to ask you again this morning. If he didn't, know he will later today, I'm sure."

"He asked me," Annabelle said then. "I said no."

"But—" Gabe started to protest and then stopped. "You're sure?"

She nodded her head emphatically and looked at Daniel and Eliza with fondness in her eyes. "I thought about it last night and decided to offer to take care of the children as a nanny instead. Adam wrote me out a letter saying he was employing me to do just that. Surely no judge would take children away from a parent who has them in the care of a nanny."

"He can't pay you," Gabe felt obliged to point out.

Annabelle nodded. "He explained that, but we don't say how much I'm being paid in the letter. He dated it and signed it. It's official."

"Well, how will you manage with no salary?"

"I don't know yet," she said. "But I'm trusting God to provide."

Gabe started to grin wider and wider. Maybe God did know what He was doing.

"You're sure you're not going to change your mind about my brother?" he asked.

"I'm very sure," she nodded.

Gabe reached across the table and offered his hand to Annabelle. "Then, would you consider marrying me instead? I think I've loved you since I saw you step down from that train."

"It's not the hat, is it?" she asked with a sudden frown.

He laughed. "The hat is lovely, but no, it's not the hat."

"And you love me?" she pressed again.

"With all my heart."

"And you know about my injuries," she said with a frown.

He nodded.

"You're not asking me because of pity, are you?"

"No," he said with a smile.

"I never thought I'd love a tall man like you," she added, beaming. "So, yes, I'll marry you."

The children let out a cheer and they all stood up.

"I think I loved you when I first saw you, too," she whispered as he took a step closer. "You see, I had this little flutter in my heart."

"Something like this?" he asked as he bent to kiss her.

Gabe decided he had a little flutter in the vicinity of his heart, too. He had a feeling he had a lot to learn about love from this woman he was going to wed.

Epilogue

Christmas, 1886

Snow had been falling all day and, now that the lanterns were lit and Daniel and Eliza were tucked into their beds, Annabelle was ready to sit down at the round table in the log house Gabe had built this past fall. She was determined to finish writing her Christmas letter to her friend Christina—the one she had been working on every evening this week. Last night she had told the other woman that she'd fallen in love with Gabe even more completely when he spent hours in this new house of theirs building cupboards that she could open easily with her injured arm. Tonight, she needed to tell about her other good news. She had Christina's last letter open in front of her and smiled as her eyes fell on the words her friend used to describe her new husband, Elijah Gable.

The door to the house opened and Annabelle looked up to see Gabe walking toward her.

"You tell Christina they're welcome to visit anytime they want," he said.

"I know she'll want to visit when the baby's born," Annabelle said as she put her hand on her belly as a reminder. They had felt the baby kick for the first time this morning.

Gabe walked over and stood behind her chair, his hands on her shoulders. "They could come for Christmas, too."

Annabelle grinned as she stood up and turned to fit herself into Gabe's arms. "Who would have thought we would be the ones to host the Dry Creek Christmas party?"

"It's your apple and raisin cake," Gabe said.

"And the children," she added.

The soldiers had talked about their Christmas visit to the old trading post until winter had turned to spring. By the time summer was over, she'd received many little bags of nuts and dried apples from the youngest of the troops.

"I warn you right now that Mrs. Baker is going to come," Gabe said as he cradled her close to him.

"Of course," Annabelle said as she smiled. "She was the first one I invited."

Gabe chuckled as he buried his head in her hair. "I invited her, too."

"Well, it is Christmas," Annabelle said, by way of excuse. "And she has started sitting in the pew beside us instead of in front of us."

They stood there together for a moment before Annabelle whispered, "I sent word to your brother, too."

Gabe nodded. "I expected as much."

"I still believe he'll come around," Annabelle said. "For the sake of the children."

"I hope he does."

They were silent then, content to be together in the warmth of their home.

Then Gabe looked down at her. "Have I told you lately how glad I am you agreed to marry me?"

"Yes, but I don't mind hearing it again," Annabelle said with a smile. She marveled that God knew which man was her own true love.

With that thought in mind, she stood on her tiptoes and kissed him.

* * * * *

Dear Reader,

I'm always grateful when you join me for one of my Christmas stories. I've written quite a few of them by now, so you may have read several of them. If you like this one, please go back and check out my other Christmas stories, starting with the first, *An Angel for Dry Creek*.

One thing I often mention in my letter at the end of a Christmas book is that this is a time of year when people experience different feelings. For some, Christmas is a hard time either because of remembered tragedy or current difficulties. If that is your situation this year, please seek out a local fellowship group. We all need the care of others over the holidays.

If you have a minute, drop me a line and let me know if you enjoyed this story. I love to hear from readers. Just go to my website at *http://www.janettronstad.com* and contact me there.

And have a joy-filled Christmas season.

Janet Tronstad

Questions for Discussion

1. It took a lot of courage to be a mail-order bride. Annabelle struggles with trusting God in the situation. What situations have you struggled to trust God in lately?

2. Gabe and Adam had a falling-out as children that has followed them into adulthood. Have you had something like this that just seems to grow worse as the years pass by? What have you done about it, if anything? What would you like to do?

3. Mrs. Baker was threatening to have the children taken away from Adam Stone. Do you think she was right or wrong? What would you have done in her place?

4. Annabelle feels more confident when she wears her hat. What makes you feel more confident? Is it all right to feel confident because of things or should our confidence come from God alone?

5. Annabelle can't do the physical work expected of wives in the Western days. Have you ever been in a situation where you have physical limitations? How does that make you feel? Did it make you turn to God or away from Him?

6. The soldiers are lonely at Christmas and come to the trading post for cake and conversation. Have you ever offered hospitality to others who were lonely over a holiday? How did that make you feel?

REQUEST YOUR FREE BOOKS!

2 FREE INSPIRATIONAL NOVELS
PLUS 2
FREE
MYSTERY GIFTS

Love Inspired
HISTORICAL
INSPIRATIONAL HISTORICAL ROMANCE

YES! Please send me 2 FREE Love Inspired® Historical novels and my 2 FREE mystery gifts (gifts are worth about $10). After receiving them, if I don't wish to receive any more books, I can return the shipping statement marked "cancel". If I don't cancel, I will receive 4 brand-new novels every month and be billed just $4.49 per book in the U.S. or $4.99 per book in Canada. That's a saving of at least 22% off the cover price. It's quite a bargain! Shipping and handling is just 50¢ per book in the U.S. and 75¢ per book in Canada.* I understand that accepting the 2 free books and gifts places me under no obligation to buy anything. I can always return a shipment and cancel at any time. Even if I never buy another book, the two free books and gifts are mine to keep forever.

102/302 IDN FEHF

Name	(PLEASE PRINT)	
Address		Apt. #
City	State/Prov.	Zip/Postal Code

Signature (if under 18, a parent or guardian must sign)

Mail to the **Reader Service**:
IN U.S.A.: P.O. Box 1867, Buffalo, NY 14240-1867
IN CANADA: P.O. Box 609, Fort Erie, Ontario L2A 5X3

Not valid for current subscribers to Love Inspired Historical books.

Want to try two free books from another series?
Call 1-800-873-8635 or visit www.ReaderService.com

* Terms and prices subject to change without notice. Prices do not include applicable taxes. Sales tax applicable in N.Y. Canadian residents will be charged applicable taxes. Offer not valid in Quebec. This offer is limited to one order per household. All orders subject to credit approval. Credit or debit balances in a customer's account(s) may be offset by any other outstanding balance owed by or to the customer. Please allow 4 to 6 weeks for delivery. Offer available while quantities last.

Your Privacy—The Reader Service is committed to protecting your privacy. Our Privacy Policy is available online at www.ReaderService.com or upon request from the Reader Service.

We make a portion of our mailing list available to reputable third parties that offer products we believe may interest you. If you prefer that we not exchange your name with third parties, or if you wish to clarify or modify your communication preferences, please visit us at www.ReaderService.com/consumerschoice or write to us at Reader Service Preference Service, P.O. Box 9062, Buffalo, NY 14269. Include your complete name and address.

LIH11B